Begin and End With You

by

A.R. Moler

Chronology of stories in the Division P universe

Braided Lives

Hell Dogs Squadron

Seeking The Balance

Falling From a Height

Zero to 165

Don't Fret the Timing

Braided Lives 2

Begin and End With You

The LD50 of Memories

Fragmentation

Braided Lives 3 (coming in 2021)

Chapter One

A gust of wind blew a few leaves across the empty road in front of Brayden Milbourne's Pathfinder. The headlights blanched some of the bigger ones pale in the darkness. Brayden's thoughts were occupied by one of his current cases. As a detective for the Richmond police department, there were always too many cases on his plate, but that was the nature of the job. Yesterday, a car with a man's body had been found in the James River, and it was still undecided whether it was suicide or homicide. He wasn't sure why his brain kept picking at the details; maybe it was the sheer curiosity of uncertainty.

It was nearly midnight as he headed home, home being a ranch style house set on a couple of nice, wooded acres west of the city. After work days often spent in the urban grunge, it was soul saving to get away from that.

Rounding a curve, Brayden slammed on the brakes, slewing the truck sideways to avoid hitting a man walking down the center of the lane. His heart pounded with the shock of the near miss as he stared out through the windshield. A thin man wearing jeans, no shirt, no shoes, stood wavering in the headlights from Brayden's truck. Probably drunk off his ass and trying to walk home. Brayden got out.

"Are you okay? I damn near hit you. You should be walking on the shoulder," said Brayden, approaching the man. The closer he got though, the more he revised his original assumption. Under the film of dirt that coated the man's face, torso and jeans, his skin was ghost white and he held himself like he was in pain.

The man stared blankly at the ground. When Brayden was within touching distance, he suddenly realized it wasn't dirt that covered the man, but blood, mostly dried but still glossy wet in a few places. The man sank to his hands and knees, head drooping forward.

"Jesus God…what the hell?" Brayden yanked a pair of nitrile gloves from his pocket and put them on, acknowledging the irony that a cop would carry a pair of gloves by habit .

Brayden's thoughts were racing as he knelt down beside the man. *There aren't any huge gaping wounds. Where did all the blood come from? How much of it is this man's and how much is someone else's?*

"Talk to me. How bad are you hurt? Tell me what happened."

The man made a faint whimper, and Brayden put a hand on the man's shoulder … Then almost yanked it back. There was something intimately familiar about touching this man. Brayden eased him into a sitting position. The glare from the headlights spot lit the man's face, and Brayden sucked in a harsh breath. It was Jamie. Jamie Ketelsen, the G-man, the CIA agent, with whom Brayden had spent a long, glorious, sex-laden weekend nearly two months ago.

"Jamie?" Brayden said. "Jamie, what the hell happened to you?"

He cupped Jamie's face in his hands. One eye socket was badly bruised and a gash above his eyebrow had obviously dripped blood down the side of his face. His lower lip was split too. Jamie stared vacantly past Brayden's shoulder. Brayden ran his hands gently down Jamie's torso, trying to figure out if there was other damage. There seemed to be shadows of bruises beneath the crust of dried blood; it was hard to tell for sure in the harsh light of the truck's headlights.

Brayden debated about calling for an ambulance versus taking Jamie directly to the hospital himself. The other man definitely seemed to be in deep shock. Calling an ambulance would involve wait time, and that was time Brayden wasn't sure he was willing to spend. There was something wrong, very wrong with Jamie; Brayden was sure in his gut. Touching Jamie had never felt like this.

"Come on, Jamie. I'm going to help you stand up and walk over to my truck," Brayden said. He stood up and carefully helped the other man to his feet. Jamie's steps were a stumbling shuffle, and Brayden wondered if it might have been easier to try to carry him.

Opening the passenger side door, Brayden eased Jamie down into the seat. He could feel Jamie trembling. How much of that was from the dropping temperature of the night and how much was pure shock? Brayden got a blanket from the rear of his SUV. He brought it back to Jamie and wrapped it around him.

Jamie finally met Brayden's gaze. He lifted a hand and touched Brayden's chest, whispering, "Help please."

Brayden carefully squeezed Jamie's fingers. "We're going to the emergency room. They'll help, I promise." He shut the door and scrambled back around the vehicle to get in. As he pulled away, he got on the radio.

"Dispatch, this is Detective Milbourne, badge number 396. I just picked up an adult white male on highway 652. It looks like he's been assaulted. Please notify a forensic unit to meet me at the St. Francis Hospital ER." Brayden flipped the switched on the bubble light on his dashboard and drove as fast as he dared.

As his truck raced through the darkness, his mind churned with memories. He and Jamie Ketelsen had met at a motorcycle charity event to raise money for one of the local cancer support groups two months ago. Brayden owned a Hayabusa, and Jamie had a sweet little Suzuki 500 GSX. They'd struck up a conversation that led to grabbing dinner. It turned out that Jamie worked for the CIA and was just recently back from a five-month operation in Syria. He had a few weeks of downtime before his next assignment.

There had been enough chemistry between them that Brayden had picked up the hints that Jamie was dropping and the night had ended in an epic liplock in the corner of the restaurant parking lot. That kiss was the hottest thing Brayden had experienced in his life… because he could feel the warm caress of Jamie's mind inside his head. He'd always known he had some of the psychic talent that ran in his family, but he'd never encountered another guy with anything similar. Jamie had it too, had it in spades.

They didn't exactly talk it out, but they both acknowledged the attraction and the talent they shared. The following weekend had been spent in bed, on the sofa, bent over the kitchen table… as they reveled in the heights that their shared link could take them to.

As the weekend ended, Jamie confessed he had a new assignment and was liable to be unavailable for at least a month, maybe more. Promises were made to get in touch as soon Jamie was free again.

Brayden cast a quick glance at Jamie's form huddled in the blanket. Who the hell had hurt Jamie like this? Was it job related?

Twenty minutes later, Brayden pulled up to the ER entrance. Staff waited with a wheelchair. As the passenger door was opened by a man in scrubs, Jamie cringed back against the seat. Brayden could feel the fear radiating from him.

"It's okay. This is the hospital. These people just want to help," said Brayden.

"Nononononono," Jamie whimpered, trying to avoid the touch of the male nurse.

Brayden put out a hand and calmly blocked the reaching hand of the nurse. "Hey listen, he's pretty traumatized. I think it would work better if you let me help him out of the truck."

"Okay, I can do that," said the nurse.

Getting out and going around to the passenger side, Brayden gently helped Jamie stand. The other man was weak and still trembling, and Brayden was thankful for the wheelchair. He doubted Jamie could walk more than a couple of steps unaided. He pushed the wheelchair inside the building and followed the nurse into a cubicle.

"The forensic people are going to need his jeans. If you could just set them aside, that would be really helpful," said Brayden.

The nurse nodded. "You can wait in the hallway. We'll let you know when we have more information."

Brayden started to leave the room, but a cry from Jamie made him turn back. Jamie was pushing against the hands of the nurse, as the nurse tried to put a blood pressure cuff around his arm.

"No! Don't touch me!" Jamie shrieked, doing his best to fight off the nurse. He kicked the wheeled stand holding the blood pressure cuff halfway across the room.

Brayden went to Jamie and dropped to one knee in front of him, reaching to take Jamie's wrists. He stopped. Here in the better lighting of the ER, he could see ligature marks under the streaks of dried blood. Instead he took hold of Jamie's fingers as gently as possible. Brayden could feel the fear and confusion seeping off Jamie in waves. "You're hurt. You have to let them look at you. I need to know how badly you're injured."

Jamie gave him a fearful blinking stare and nodded slightly.

"I think it might work a whole lot better if you let me stay here beside him," Brayden said to the nurse.

***

Maybe it looked funny to be holding another guy's hand, but at the moment Brayden didn't give a shit. He'd figured out fifteen minutes ago that doing so was the only thing keeping Jamie from going totally ape shit.

10

Jamie was stripped and cleaned up enough to begin assessment of his injuries. There were numerous bruises all over Jamie's body: torso, legs, arms, and face. There were also a number of cuts and abrasions. His ankles bore the same sort of ligature marks as his wrists, and by the time enough dried blood was removed, there were finger-shaped bruises around his throat too. Thankfully there was nothing to indicate sexual assault.

While they waited for X-rays to be developed, the nurse returned to the cubicle to take information. "I need your name and social security number. We'll figure out about the insurance in a little while," she said.

Jamie gave the woman a blank look and just shook his head a little.

"It's okay, just give them the information," said Brayden.

"Dunno," whispered Jamie.

"You don't know your name? Or you don't know your social?" the nurse asked

"Name."

"Um... okay…" The nurse looked sort of mystified.

Brayden volunteered the limited information he knew. "I know his name. We met a couple of months ago. His name is Jamie Ketelsen. I have no idea about his social security number or physical address, but I have an email address and I know he's employed by the CIA."

"Okay, that's a start. I'm going to go talk to the doctor about the memory problem." The nurse left again.

Jamie gave Brayden a bleary, glazed stare. "Who are you?"

Brayden heaved a deep breath. This kept getting weirder and more complicated. "My name is Brayden Milbourne. We met about two months ago at a motorcycle rally for charity. We're …friends." It was a simpler thing to say than lovers, because he wasn't even sure they knew each other well enough to qualify as that. And fuck-buddies was probably too extreme an idea to dump on Jamie at the moment. "I'm a detective for the Richmond police department."

The nurse returned. "One of the police department's forensic people is here."

"Send them in. We have to have documentation," Brayden said.

The forensic tech was a black woman named Samantha Reed that Brayden knew from their interaction at quite a few crime scenes. She took several dozen photos of Jamie's injuries, scraped under his fingernails for trace DNA evidence, and bagged his bloodstained jeans. There hadn't been any other clothing, not even underwear. That in itself was disturbing.

"Do we have a suspect yet for who assaulted him?" asked Samantha.

"No, I don't think so. Jamie? Do you remember anything about what happened?" Brayden laid a hand on Jamie's leg.

Jamie shook his head. His expression was a tight grimace of denial.

"Just mark it as unknown at this point," said Brayden.

As Samantha left, the doctor came back in. "Are you family?"

"No," said Brayden. "A friend, but I'm also the police detective that found him. I need some information on his injuries for the assault report."

"Very well." The doctor faced Jamie. "I got the X-rays back. You have hairline fractures of two ribs and another on the orbit next to your eye. Nothing's out of alignment, and they're not in places we could cast anyway. The one around your eye troubles me a little, because the nurse said you were experiencing memory loss, more than just the few hours surrounding the trauma. You almost certainly have a concussion. I'd like to send you for a CAT scan just to make sure there's no more serious brain injury, but first I'm going to have you do a quick little neurological test."

Jamie had distinct difficulty standing upright and still if his eyes were closed, Brayden noted. His coordination seemed a little off too. The touch your nose and lift one foot commands given by the doctor reminded Brayden of a sobriety test. Jamie wouldn't have passed.

***

Lying on the table, wearing nothing but a skimpy hospital gown and trying to hold as still as possible for the CAT scan, Jamie closed his eyes. Who was he? That guy Milbourne had provided him with a name and said they were friends. It felt like there was more to it than that, but Jamie couldn't figure out why. Milbourne made him feel safe. Was that because the guy was a cop? There had to be something else, but every poke at his missing memory just made his head hurt worse. At some point, he needed to sleep. His entire body ached. Based on what he had seen of himself, he was covered in bruises and scrapes.

Somebody had done this to him. A car accident wouldn't have left him mostly naked without any ID. For no good reason he could fathom, he felt he was still in danger. Whoever was responsible might come back and decide to finish the job.

When the CAT scan was finished, he was taken back to the exam room from earlier. Brayden was there waiting for him. Jamie felt unexpectedly relieved.

The female nurse who had taken Jamie to radiology helped him back on the gurney. "It'll be a little bit until they get the CAT scan read."

Jamie nodded. He wanted to reach for Brayden. More than that, he wanted to curl up against Brayden and just beg the man to hold him. How twisted was that? It had to be a symptom of whatever was messed up in his head. A long burst of trembling shook him, and Jamie clenched his hand on the light blanket the nurse had covered his legs with. The shaking ramped up the aches of his body.

"When they get around to releasing you, I have a duffle bag with some spare clothes in the back of my SUV. I know they'll be too big, and the shoes won't fit, but it'll do until we can figure something else out," said Brayden. He placed a hand on Jamie's arm. "Do you want me to ask somebody for another blanket?"

"N-no. Not really c-cold, just…" Jamie hugged his arms to his chest.

"Hey, it's okay. You've had a really shitty experience, but we're getting this under control."

Jamie noticed the choice of words, specifically the "we" part. Brayden seemed to be putting a fair bit of effort into helping him. Exactly what kind of friend was Brayden? How far could Jamie trust him? How far had he trusted him in the past? Jamie curled up on the gurney and closed his eyes, feeling overwhelmed.

It was another half an hour before the doctor returned. "The CAT scan doesn't show any abnormalities, but I'm going to give you a referral to a neurologist. I suspect the memory thing and the coordination problems will clear up in the next day or two, but if they don't, especially if they don't, you should contact the neurologist. If we discharge you, do you have someone to stay with? With the head injury, you shouldn't be alone for the next twenty-four hours at least."

"I'll keep an eye on him," said Brayden.

"Fair enough. One of the nurses will get the discharge paperwork together. It'll include some things to watch out for."

***

It was getting close to dawn by the time Brayden got home with Jamie in tow. As they walked into the house, Brayden noticed just how long his jeans were on Jamie. They were a good four inches too long, not to mention that the belt was probably the only thing keeping them up around Jamie's narrower hips. One

15

arm around Jamie's waist, one hand under his elbow, Brayden guided Jamie's unsteady steps.

"I suggest some food, then some sleep. No offense, but you look awful," said Brayden.

Jamie nodded.

"Come on into the kitchen. How does eggs and toast strike you?"

"Fine."

Brayden took him to the kitchen table. "Have a seat. It won't take very long." He took the egg carton from the refrigerator. "Do you want to wait until you've had some sleep to see how much of your memory comes back? Or do you want me to call the CIA and see what I can find out?"

Jamie blearily looked like he was mulling the question over. "I think I'd rather wait, at least a few more hours."

"Scrambled or fried?"

"Huh? Oh, it doesn't matter, whatever's easiest. "

It took less than ten minutes to make breakfast. Brayden handed Jamie a plate and sat down across from him.

"Have I been here before?" Jamie asked.

"Yes, once, not quite two months ago. Does it look familiar?" Brayden was hopeful.

"No."

"That's okay."

After they finished eating, Brayden showed Jamie back to the spare bedroom. There were a batch of boxes stowed along one wall, but the room also contained a bed and a nightstand.

"Just to forewarn you, the hospital's instructions say to wake you every couple of hours until late this evening. Do you want something more comfortable than my way-too-big jeans to sleep in?"

Jamie grimaced slightly. "I feel like I've already asked a hell of a lot of you, but yes."

"I'll go grab some sweats. Don't feel like you're taking advantage of me or something, I volunteered to take care of you. There must be some kind of fairy godmother keeping an eye on you as it is. If it hadn't been me that found you, the hospital would still be scratching their heads on what to do with you."

Brayden went into his own bedroom dresser and pulled out a pair of sweat pants. That weekend, that magnificent weekend, Jamie had slept in Brayden's bed and there hadn't been much clothing the whole two and half days. He went back to the other bedroom.

Jamie was seated on the bed, hands hanging limp between his knees, head tipped forward. He looked up as Brayden came in.

"These are going to be too big also, but it's the best I can offer." Brayden handed the sweats to Jamie.

"Thanks." Jamie stood up and immediately grabbed at the wall, to steady himself.

Brayden reached out and took hold of Jamie's upper arms. "Hey, careful. Maybe I should help." Jamie gave him an uncertain look, and Brayden could sense exhausted confusion. They stood immobile for several seconds.

"I'm guessing we're more than just friends," Jamie said eventually.

Brayden felt torn about how he should describe their relationship. "Yes and no. It's complicated. I was completely truthful when I said we met at a motorcycle gig. We had dinner, and spent some time talking about bikes and traveling and other crap. But… the following weekend, we… uh… hooked up and did the wild thing… way more than once."

Jamie gave him a lopsided grin.

"But listen, no pressure. You're having memory problems, got beat all to hell, and look like you're about dead on your feet. Right now, you need some rest. So just let me help you change and you can get some sleep. Talking about the rest of it can wait."

Brayden gently helped Jamie strip off the T-shirt and over-sized jeans. There were still traces of dried blood in a lot of places and Brayden was tempted to suggest a shower, but he didn't think Jamie could handle standing up that long right now. Helping Jamie pull up the sweats and tie the drawstring, he noticed that some of the bruises were different colors. That indicated to him that Jamie had been beaten over the span of at least three days, maybe more. Wow, that idea tied the knots of concern in Brayden's stomach a little tighter. Combined with the lack of clothing, ID and such, all the facts hinted at a scenario far darker and more complicated than a conventional robbery/assault. His thoughts circled around to the CIA and god knows what op Jamie had been on since the last time they saw each other.

Jamie sank down onto the bed and drew a blanket up over himself.

***

Getting woken up every two hours sucked. The sun was beginning to set as Brayden woke Jamie yet again.

"It's past six. Are you hungry?" asked Brayden as he sat on the edge of the bed.

"Yeah, some."

"Are you feeling any better?"

"My head doesn't ache so bad, but everything else. Ugh." Jamie made a half-hearted attempt to stretch. "Unh, God, ow."

"Guess all those bruised muscles stiffened up. I'm not in the mood to cook, and there's only two places that deliver in this area. So we're limited to pizza or Chinese. Do you have a preference?"

"Chinese, I guess."

"I'll go hunt up the menu. Come on out to the den when you're ready, but feel free to give me a yell if you need a hand. The bathroom's at the end of the hallway."

Getting out of bed made Jamie feel like he was a hundred years old and drew several groans of pain from him. He shuffled off to the bathroom and took care of business, then stood looking in the mirror. He had wavy, medium brown hair, cut corporate short. It stood up in all directions from his sleeping. Brown eyes looked back at him. He was a good hand span shorter than Brayden and skinnier. Brayden probably outweighed him by a good twenty-five to thirty pounds of hard, heavy muscle.

He examined his black eye critically. The bruising was deeper on the outer edge of the socket. He suspected that meant somebody had hit him with a fist. He ran his tongue along his damaged lip. It tasted faintly of blood. It was probably the result of another fist to the face. Why the hell didn't he remember somebody beating the shit out of him?

A wave of dizziness washed through him as he was leaving the bathroom, and he wondered if he was going to end up face down on the hallway carpet. He made his way out to the den, one hand on the wall.

Brayden was in the den sitting on the sofa. "I found the menu. Figure out what you want, and I'll call it in." He handed the menu to Jamie.

Jamie sat on the sofa and looked at the menu… And blinked and looked again. He could see squiggles he knew must be lettering but they meant nothing. He ran a fingertip over the surface of the thin cardboard, tracing a curvy line. He was an adult. Adults knew how to read. Maybe it was in a different language?

"I can't read Chinese," Jamie said.

Brayden raised an eyebrow, then grinned. "Funny. Does that mean you can't decide?"

"No… I … I don't know what it says. Is it in English?"

Brayden suddenly sobered. "You're serious?"

"Yeah."

"Yes, it's in English." Brayden pointed to the lettering across the top. "King Panda Palace."

"If you say so. It just looks like squiggles and lines."

"Uh… wow… Is this part of the memory problem?"

"I don't know. I'm guessing I could read before all this."

"Yeah, just fine, as far as I know. Last time I saw you, you wrote down your email address for me and I remember you reading me a piece of an article off a website about some weird new hybrid motorcycle."

"What the hell else has gotten wiped out of my head?" Jamie clenched his fists in frustration and crossed his arms. He grimaced; his arms put pressure on his cracked ribs when he did that. He let his hands fall into his lap.

"It hasn't even been a full twenty-four hours since I found you. I think you're going to have to give it some time."

"Tell me everything you know about me," Jamie begged.

"It's not a lot. Like I said before, we'd only seen each other two weekends, and the first one was mostly just casual chit-chat stuff."

"Tell me about the motorcycle," Jamie said.

"You have a little black and red 500cc Suzuki GSX. You've only had it a couple of years."

"Where is it?"

"The motorcycle? I have no idea. At your house or apartment, I guess," Brayden replied.

"Where do I live?"

"Rockville, Maryland; I think that's what you told me."

"Do I own a car?"

Brayden shrugged. "I don't know. It didn't come up in conversation."

"Do I have family? Brothers? Sisters? Parents?" Jamie asked.

"No idea."

"You said I work for the CIA. Am I a field agent?"

"I think so. You said you'd spent five months in Syria shortly before we met. I ragged on you and said you were making it up about being a spook, so you showed me your ID, and told me that you only carried it when you were in the States. Which brings me back to my earlier question, do you want me to try to contact someone there?"

"Not yet."

Brayden gazed at him for a long moment before he asked, "Why?"

"A feeling. A weird bad feeling that I have no good reason for."

"Do you think the CIA did something to you?"

"No, no, I can't explain it. It was… someone…there was someone … Fuck, it feels like I can almost maybe see somebody giving me an assignment and… then nothing." Jamie ran his hands through his hair, wishing he could stick his fingers into his skull and dig something useful out of his brain.

"Don't push it. Why don't we focus on dinner? Do you want me to read the menu to you?"

Jamie sighed. "Yes."

***

Comfortably full of pork fried rice and General Tso's chicken, Brayden glanced at Jamie in the light of the TV. Jamie's head was resting against Brayden's shoulder, his eyes only half open. There was a Monday night football game playing, but neither of them was paying more than scant attention.

Jamie's fingers were tracing tiny paths along the top of Brayden's leg and Brayden could sense a deep-seated worry gnawing at Jamie. It bothered him that someone he had begun to care about was this close to desolate.

He slid back into the corner of the sofa and crooked a finger at Jamie. "Come here." Jamie scooted close, and Brayden pulled Jamie against his chest, stretching his legs out along the couch so Jamie was mostly on top of him. He ran a hand down Jamie's back. "We'll figure it out. I promise."

23

Jamie's head rested on Brayden's collarbone. "How come touching you feels like the only thing that's holding me together?"

"It's the psychic thing I think."

"You're psychic?"

"A little. It runs in my family, but hey, so are you, maybe even more than me. We didn't really do any more than agree we both knew we had it that weekend."

"Is that why we ended up in bed so fast?"

Brayden chuckled. "I don't know. Maybe. Or maybe I'm just easy."

Jamie looked up at him and touched a fingertip to Brayden's mouth. "You don't strike me as a guy that does casual very well."

"That sounds disturbingly reminiscent of something my brother said to me. He thinks I view the world a little too black and white."

"You don't get along with him?" Jamie asked.

"No, I do, after a fashion. There are just some things we butt heads about," said Brayden.

Jamie squirmed a little until he was flat on top of Brayden and lay there just breathing for several minutes.

Brayden's arms stole the rest of the way around Jamie and hugged him gently, resting a cheek on the top of Jamie's head.

The Jamie he knew had a broad aggressive streak, a wicked
sense of humor, and leaned toward being an adrenaline junkie.
The Jamie he held in his arms felt broken and damaged, and
Brayden longed for a way to put him back together. The first rule
of fixing things was figuring out what was wrong. The physical
damage was pretty obvious, from the bruises to the cracked
bones to the marks left on Jamie's wrists and ankles. Somebody
had bound him, either to make it easier to torture him or to
prevent escape. The mental damage was harder to figure out.
Brayden hoped it would sort itself out soon.

"I can feel you analyzing me," Jamie whispered.

"Does that bother you?"

"No. Somebody needs to help me get my head back together.
You're the best candidate."

An idea occurred to Brayden. Maybe he had a way to stir up
Jamie's missing memory. "When I was a kid, my brother and my
sister and I used to play a game. We all knew we had something
a little extra and we'd try to purposely sneak a peek at what each
other was thinking about. Usually it was dumb stuff like the fact
that Kylie stole cookies out of the cookie jar before dinner or that
Steve swiped one of Dad's Playboy mags. Maybe I can nudge
one of the blank spots and jog your memory a little more
directly. What do you think?"

"Yeah, sure. It sounds like it's worth a try."

"Just close your eyes and relax." Brayden stared at the TV
screen, letting the images he saw wash away most of his

conscious thoughts. He opened himself fully to Jamie's presence, feeling Jamie's mind touching his own.

Jamie's ribs hurt and his head, and everything else too. ... *I need to dose him up with some Tylenol soon. If I skim along the surface, maybe I'll notice something he's ignoring. When people aren't upset, their presence feels smooth and curvy. What the fuck is that?*

Brayden was shocked by the sensation. It reminding him of examining bullet wounds punched into flesh. They were gaping torn holes; if it had been physical Brayden would have expected blood to still be seeping. Jamie whimpered and flinched where he lay on top of Brayden's body. Brayden had never felt damage like this before, not even when he had to interview witnesses to murder.

"Shh, shh. It's okay," Brayden soothed, rubbing Jamie's back and brushing a kiss on his forehead. He had no idea what to do. Part of him was astonished that Jamie was as functional as he was.

"Oh God … fuck … that hurt." Jamie moaned.

"I'm sorry. Jesus, I'm so sorry. I didn't mean to hurt you," Brayden whispered.

"S'okay … it was just kind of like digging gravel out of road rash."

"Enh…I didn't think just nosing around would hurt. Do you want me to help you get up and let you put some space between us?" He was uncertain if continuing to hold Jamie this close was painful.

"No, not really. Except when you started poked around there, touching you makes me feel better. Less like I'm just totally going to come unglued. I know that probably sounds crazy from a guy you only halfway know. Lying here with you, having your arms around me, I feel almost safe." Jamie nuzzled his face against the side of Brayden's neck.

As Brayden's nose was pressed along Jamie's hairline, he realized Jamie smelled of sweat and blood and hospital antiseptics. "Are you up for a shower? I thought about suggesting one earlier, but you were about dead on your feet."

"I'm kind of intermittently dizzy, but yeah, that might be a good idea."

"I can help, but only if you're okay with it. I know it's got to be really weird knowing that we got naked and fucked each other stupid, and you don't remember any of it."

"I trust you. This thing between us, even despite my totally messed up brain, it feels right."

***

One hand braced on the tiled wall, Jamie watched brown-red water swirling down the drain. He'd been under the illusion that the hospital had cleaned him up more. It had seemed like minute after minute of wiping and touching had occurred, none of it comfortable, and if hadn't been for Brayden's hand holding his in the ER, he'd probably have started screaming.

Brayden's fingers rubbed gently through Jamie's hair, turning the shampoo into foam. "Are doing okay?"

"Yeah…How much of this is my blood?"

"I'm not sure. The gash above your eye and the split lip probably bloodied up your face and chest some. And the scrapes across knee and elbow contributed, but the rest…I don't know."

Jamie looked up into Brayden's face. Brayden's expression was sober. He had wide cheekbones and strong, square jaw. His sandy brown hair was cut military short. "Then whose blood is it?"

"I don't know that either. You have defensive wounds on your hands and forearms. The ligature marks on your wrists and ankles are both bruised and scabbed. Somebody tied you down and beat the crap out of you. I can only guess that you either were let loose long enough to make an escape, or that you fought your way free."

"Who? Where and what the hell did they want from me?"

"I wish I had answers for you."

Jamie let his head hang forward, and Brayden curled an arm around him, pulling him close. Brayden's body was wider than Jamie's, all bulky muscle, dusted lightly by body hair. It apparently didn't matter to Jamie's libido that there was no memory of sex with this man, a thread of arousal snaked through him. A thread was the extent of it though, he still ached too badly for his cock to do more than think about the idea.

Brayden's cock on the other hand hung heavy and slightly flushed, not hard but definitely capable of heading that direction. It was a nice package too, and Jamie wondered how it would feel in his hand.

"Later," whispered Brayden. "When there's a chance you might enjoy it." His hands smoothed soap gently over Jamie's chest and arms. "Let's focus on getting all this blood off of you."

The slick skim of Brayden's big hands across Jamie's skin was a mixed blessing of sensations. Jamie enjoyed the touch until Brayden's fingers crossed particularly painful bruises. Every time it happened, he flinched and Brayden would lift his hand for a moment. They both knew enduring the little zings of pain was a necessary evil to getting fully clean.

"Once we're done with this, I was thinking maybe we should make a quick trip out to get you some clothes that fit. What do you think?" asked Brayden.

"That's probably a good idea."

Chapter Two

In Wal-mart, Jamie tried on jeans and T-shirts. He had to guess at the size, estimating a waist a few inches smaller than Brayden's and definitely a shorter inseam.

Coming out of the dressing room, he spied Brayden waiting a few feet away. "I think these will do." He held up two pair of jeans and three T-shirts.

"Good. You need sneakers too. I grabbed some socks and underwear." He pointed at the items in the shopping cart. "It's the first time I think I've ever picked out underwear for anybody but myself."

Jamie made a little snort of laughter. "So, boxers or briefs?"

"I went with tighty whities because that's what you were wearing that weekend. If you change your mind, we can always come buy something else."

A trip to the shoe section required Jamie to stand on the mat with sizes marked on it. That was profoundly weird. What adult doesn't know their own shoe size? Nine seemed like a good match, and Brayden handed him a pair of average-looking, white running shoes.

"You better try them on too, in case you decide you need a different size," suggested Brayden.

Jamie glanced around to find a place to sit. There was a short bench at the end of the aisle. He sat, stuck his foot in one of the shoes and picked up the laces… and realized he had no clue what to do with them. He stole a glance at Brayden's sneakers. They were tied in what looked like the usual way, but Jamie had no idea how to make his match.

"Too tight?" asked Brayden.

"No," Jamie answered slowly. "I, uh, I can't tie them."

"Is there something wrong with the laces?"

"No. I mean I don't know how to tie them."

Brayden gave him a solemn, concerned look. "I'm guessing that's something else that got deleted from your memory. Stay put." He walked down the aisle and returned with another box.

When Jamie took the box from Brayden's hand, he saw sneakers with Velcro tabs. "I thought they only made these for little kids."

"Nope. If they fit, we'll buy both pair and you can wear the Velcro ones for a few days while you relearn how to tie the other ones."

***

Driving back home, Brayden glanced at Jamie, who was staring out the window with a tight expression on his face. Brayden suspected physical pain was only half the problem.

"We're coming up on the spot where I found you. I was on my way home. Do you want to stop and have a look around?" Brayden asked. "It's not quite as late as it was last night."

"Yes."

31

Brayden pulled over onto the shoulder. "It was right along here. I came around the corner and nearly ran you down. Do you think you were just following the road?"

"Maybe. I have a kind of hazy memory of being here and trying to get somewhere, somewhere safe."

"Do you have any idea how far you walked?"

Jamie looked along the road in both directions. "No, not really. It seemed like a long way, but with my head so messed up it could have been less than a mile."

"Okay, think about walking along the road. Was the sun up?"

"Yes. It was daylight at some point, but I'm not sure it was this road. I… there might have been a car."

"Were you driving? Were you a passenger? Or did it just drive past you?" Brayden prompted, trying to see if he could inspire some sliver of memory.

"I don't think I was driving. … There was… water," Jamie replied.

"It didn't rain last night."

"That's the best I can do."

"Hey, it's good. You remember a snip. Want to take a walk? We'll just go back past the curve a ways and see if anything looks familiar," Brayden said.

Jamie nodded and climbed out of the car, then stood hesitantly with one hand on the trunk.

Brayden walked around the car to stand beside him. "Are you still dizzy?"

"A little. It comes and goes."

"Do you want me to hang on to you?"

"Yeah, maybe. Walking in the store was level and well lighted and all, out here…"

Brayden gently wound an arm around Jamie's waist and they walked slowly up the edge of the road.

A couple hundred feet along, Jamie paused and turned around, looking back toward the curve. "I remember the curve… except it was daytime and … I think maybe I was on a motorcycle…"

"The weekend we spent together, you came to my place and you were on your bike. Anything else?" Jamie stood motionless and Brayden could feel the anxious tension in Jamie as the man wracked his brain for pieces of memory.

"No. Just that fragment. A two or three second blip of my life."

"Every bit puts you a little closer. Do you think you were heading toward my place last night?" Brayden asked.

"I don't know. I suppose it's possible. If I'd been there before, maybe my subconscious knew it was someplace familiar."

"Do you want to walk any farther?"

"No." Jamie closed his eyes. "The road feels like it's doing this slow tilt-a-whirl thing."

"Let's go back to the car. You've been up and around for several hours now. The hospital instructions said get plenty of rest for the concussion, and we're probably pushing the envelope here."

***

"You should probably get some sleep," said Brayden as they came into the house through the kitchen door. Jamie watched Brayden toss his keys on the kitchen counter and wondered if there was someplace where he did something similar, someplace he called home.

Maybe it was the fatigue, or maybe it was the concussion, but Jamie found himself fighting hard against the urge to just sit down on the floor and shake.

Brayden took hold of one of Jamie's shoulder. "Damn, I think we really did push too hard. Come on, you need to go to bed." He guided Jamie in the direction of the spare room.

Halfway there, Jamie blurted out. "Can I sleep with you? I'm too tired for anything to happen. I just don't… I need to not be alone." Brayden paused and Jamie could sense the long careful appraisal he was being given. "I know that sounds pathetically like some kid who's scared of the dark, but I feel like there's weird, nasty crap crawling in the back of my brain… I just need you close."

Brayden cupped his hands around Jamie's face. "I didn't want to push you. I know you don't remember the things we did. I didn't want to make you uncomfortable. If sleeping with me, makes you feel better though, I'm good with that."

34

They went into the master bedroom. There was a queen-sized bed with a quilt on it, creamy white with big green leaves in various shades. Brayden pulled back the blankets. Jamie stripped, fingers fumbling with the belt and the zipper on the borrowed clothes. The shower earlier had made the aches in his body lessen, but now the pain was back in full force.

Brayden took Jamie's hand and laid a pair of tablets in it. "Tylenol. The hospital instructions say no aspirin or ibuprofen for three days." He handed Jamie a glass of water.

Jamie took the meds and sank onto the bed. It took another couple of minutes for Brayden to undress, turn off the light, and slide in beside him. Jamie lay very still, feeling his own pulse slamming dully through his body. Close wasn't good enough, he hurt with the need for touch the same way his bruises and cracked ribs hurt physically. Brayden's presence felt like a pool of stillness inches away. Reaching out, Jamie brushed his fingertips against Brayden's arm.

"I don't know why I keep thinking I'm going to do something to creep you out when it's pretty obvious you need to touch me about like you need to breathe," Brayden murmured. He rolled on his side and pulled Jamie carefully against his body.

Pressed together from shoulder to thigh, with Brayden's arm gently wrapped around him, Jamie immediately felt like he was no longer hanging off the edge of some invisible cliff. He could smell Brayden's skin, soap, and a hint of male musk. He pressed his mouth against the base of Brayden's throat. The pressure against his split lip was uncomfortable but he didn't care.

Brayden tucked his chin and kissed Jamie's forehead, his nose, and then slanted his lips to kiss the corner of Jamie's mouth, mostly avoiding the injured spot.

Exhaustion sucked at Jamie. He nestled tighter against Brayden and let sleep drag him under.

***

Somebody was tearing things inside his head. Pushing, ripping, hunting for facts. The pain was excruciating and he wanted to grab the sides of his skull as he screamed, but his hands were bound behind him.

"Jamie! Jamie! Wake the fuck up!"

He sucked in an agonized gasp as he realized somebody was shaking him. Jamie sat up, heart pounding so hard it hurt. He was immediately pulled against a warm body. Brayden. One arm held him tight, a hand stroked through his hair.

"Jesus, Jamie. You were screaming and I couldn't get you to wake up," Brayden whispered. He was placing feather light kisses down the side of Jamie's face.

Breathing hurt too, mostly because Jamie was panting so hard it pulled at his cracked ribs. It took a long couple of minutes before he caught his breath and his pulse slowed. He rubbed at his wrists. The fact that he could do so easily added another layer of relief.

"Somebody was hurting you bad..." Brayden said.

"Uh-huh," was all Jamie could get out.

"I couldn't see a face, only that someone was doing their damnedest to tear apart your mind."

"Huh? Wha'? You saw my nightmare?" Jamie asked.

"Snips. Impressions. Half memories. I have this funky ass blend of a little telepathy and a little empathy and dash of clairvoyance. Not enough of any one thing to be really good at it."

Jamie swallowed hard. "He wanted…something… from me."

"He?"

"It was a guy, and my hands were tied behind my back. I think he was behind me, but I'm not absolutely sure about that."

"Every piece fits into the puzzle someplace. Was the person that beat you the same person that messed with your head?" Brayden's hands rubbed gently along Jamie's back.

"Uh, I don't think so, but I couldn't tell you anything about them either."

"One step at a time. Fact one, we know you were held against your will and tortured. Two, there were probably at least two separate people involved, and one was known to be male. Three, it's likely you were transported in a car at some point."

"That makes it sound so cut and dried."

"Sorry," whispered Brayden. "I know it doesn't feel that way to you. Sometimes it's hard to turn off the cop side of my brain."

Jamie snuggled tight against Brayden's body. Maybe snuggling wasn't the best option for his banged up ribs, but he wanted to be against the warmth of Brayden's skin.

Chapter Three

"Hey, Milbourne, the captain was looking for you," called Simmons down the hallway of the precinct building.

Brayden stopped. Why the hell would the captain want to see him first thing on the shift? That didn't bode exactly well.

"Great. What'd I fuck up this time?" Brayden asked as Simmons approached him. Simmons was a short, stocky, blond man with a penchant for loud ties.

"I have no idea. It didn't sound like he was on the warpath, so maybe it's something simple."

Walking down the corridor and around the corner, Brayden stopped and knocked lightly on the open door of the office there. The captain was sitting behind his desk, surrounded by paperwork. A black man in his fifties, Captain Calvin Dean had been in charge for nearly a decade.

"You wanted to see me, sir?" Brayden asked.

"Yeah, that assault victim you picked up the other night, somebody or other Ketelsen? One of the forensic people says you know him personally."

"Yes."

"I'm taking you off the car in the river case," Dean stated.

"Uh, okay, why?" Brayden couldn't see a connection between the two separate statements.

"Forensics started processing the car. It's looking like a homicide."

"Why does that disqualify me for working on it?"

"Ketelsen's wallet was found in the car," the Captain said.

"In case you've forgotten, he's a victim. I think he was abducted. Samantha processed him at the hospital. He has ligature marks on his ankles and wrists, and defensive wounds on his arms and hands. Wouldn't it make a whole lot more sense to assume the guy in the car was responsible for kidnapping Jamie? If, and I think there's a pretty big if, Jamie did kill that guy, it sounds like there'd be a good case for self defense."

"Only some of the facts are in. At the moment, it could go either way. Ketelsen might be a victim, or he might be the perp. There was something in the hospital report about amnesia. That sounds just a trifle too convenient. Is he staying with you?"

"Yes."

"You might want to rethink that."

"Jamie Ketelsen is not a murderer, He is, however, a CIA agent," Brayden snapped.

"The CIA doesn't operate domestically. You can stay in the loop information wise, but it's hands off on the investigation. In the meantime, I want him brought in for an interview."

"When?"

"This afternoon would be good."

"Yes, sir." Brayden headed straight to forensics after he left the captain's office. He wanted details on why Jamie was being eyeballed for murder. In the forensics wing, he hunted down Samantha

"What's up?" she asked.

"Talk to me about the body in the river and Jamie Ketelsen's assault. How are they connected?" he said.

"The vehicle processing crew found a wallet with Ketelsen's driver's license in it, issued in Maryland. It also has a second driver's license. Same picture but the name is Jacob McCoy. That one is from California."

"Keep going."

"Both check out as valid." Samantha crossed her arms.

"Jamie's CIA. The McCoy one is probably a cover identity," said Brayden.

"The M.E. did the autopsy on the guy in the car. COD wasn't drowning. He was stabbed. There's no sign of the weapon. Blood pooling and all suggests he was put in the car very shortly after he was killed."

"But beyond the wallet and the ID, there's nothing to verify that Jamie is the one who killed him?" Brayden said.

"True, so far," said Samantha.

"You saw Jamie's injuries. You saw the ligature marks on his wrists and ankles. He's a victim. Don't you think it's possible that this guy was transporting Jamie after his abduction?"

"It's possible. Right now we're just following the evidence trail."

"How 'bout an ID on the river guy?" Brayden asked, hoping for good news.

"Nothing yet. There's an implication that his dental work was not done in the U.S."

"I guess the river washed away any DNA evidence?"

"We haven't located anything usable so far. We do have the jeans Ketelsen was wearing and the scraping from his fingernails," Samantha said.

"And if the blood matches the body, I guess that doesn't look good."

"Not especially."

***

The TV was showing a news clip about Syria when Jamie heard the door open. "What are you doing home so soon?" he asked as Brayden came into the room.

"I was sent to… bring you in." Brayden looked stressed and stood with his hands in the pockets of his slacks.

"Why?"

"The captain wants you interviewed. They found your wallet in a car that also contained a dead body."

Jamie glanced at the TV. One of the talking heads was babbling about civil unrest and political prisoners. For just a moment, the image of standing in a street with Arabic signs on the shops flitted through his head. Then he wrenched his thoughts back to what Brayden had just said.

"Do they think I was in that car at some point?" he asked.

Brayden's lips pressed together in a taut line. "There's speculation that you killed the man found in the car. Listen, try not to worry too much. It's all just circumstantial evidence at this point." He sat down and laid a hand on Jamie's leg.

"What if I did kill him? It's not like I have an alibi or even any memory of … 98% of my life. If I'm CIA, it's stands to reason I would actually know how to kill. What kind of gun was used?"

A little hint of a smile tugged at Brayden's mouth. "You're better off not knowing. There's some complicating factors in all this too."

Jamie sat up straighter. "Like?"

"They found two different driver's licenses with your picture on them in the wallet."

"Wouldn't that be a fairly usual thing for a CIA operative?"

"That's what I said to the captain." Brayden squeezed Jamie's leg gently. "Let's get this over with, then I think we need to devote some serious consideration to calling the CIA."

***

This wasn't a booking, Brayden was told. Jamie was a "person of interest" regarding the murder of the as yet unidentified male body from the car in the river. It was a mixed blessing type of situation in Brayden's opinion. Obviously there wasn't enough evidence to charge Jamie but he wasn't in the clear either. Brayden waited in the hallway. Jamie was about to be led in the direction of the interrogation rooms. A uniformed officer grabbed Jamie's arm. Jamie flinched and tried to pull away.

"I can walk," said Jamie. There was distinct edge of tension in his voice.

"I'm sure you can." The officer tightened his grip.

Brayden was highly tempted to yell down the hall at the officer, but held his tongue, trying not to complicate the whole process. Then the whole thing went to hell in a hand basket.

The officer was apparently in a pissy mood and not willing to tolerate Jamie's objections to manhandling. He grabbed Jamie more firmly and spun him around to face the wall. The officer yanked out his handcuffs and used them on Jamie .

Jamie went bat-shit.

In the span of about two seconds, Jamie was thrashing and struggling. He kicked the man who had handcuffed him and drove the cop against the wall with a hard thrust of his shoulder. Another officer dashed to help. Vicious kicks and thrashing and head butts, Jamie fought the cops with surprising efficiency. A third cop was joining in as Brayden began sprinting up the hallway. They took Jamie kicking, screaming and fighting to the floor.

"Leave him the hell alone!" Brayden screamed. "He's got broken bones and a head injury."

By the time Brayden fell to his knees, pushing and shoving at the other men, Jamie lay motionless on the tile. His nose was bleeding and the gash above his eye had torn open again. His eyes were only half open.

"You fucking morons! He's a victim. Somebody tied him up and beat the shit out of him! And you cuff him?" On the floor, Jamie twitched, one leg, one shoulder, head banging against the floor. "Oh hell, he's seizing! Get these cuffs off him. Call an ambulance NOW!"

Uncertainly, one of the cops put a handcuff key in Brayden's hand. Brayden swiftly unlocked the cuffs and pulled Jamie up into his arms, protecting his head from further impact. The rhythmic, uncontrolled motion of Jamie's arms and head went on for a good two minutes or more before Jamie finally went limp.

Brayden checked his pulse. It was fast and weak, but Jamie seemed to be breathing okay. Blood, drool, and snot coated one side of Jamie's face. "Hey you, get me something so I can try and stop the bleeding," Brayden yelled at one of the onlookers.

Somebody brought him paper towels and a first aid kit. He wiped away the worst of the blood and tore open some 4x4's to hold against the bloody gash on Jamie's forehead. Beyond that there was very little he could do for Jamie until the EMTs got there. He simple held Jamie, who was half sprawled across his legs, head drooping bonelessly against Brayden's chest.

The EMTs got there a few minutes later. After checking vitals and bandaging the head wound, they loaded Jamie onto the stretcher.

Jamie was beginning to show signs of regaining consciousness, eyelids fluttering and one hand reaching out.

Brayden took his hand. "Just lie still. You had a seizure, and the EMTs are here to take you to the hospital."

Jamie's eyes opened about halfway and gazed in Brayden's general direction, but Brayden wasn't sure if the man was coherent enough to register what was going on.

***

Damn, damn, damn. Back in the ER, Brayden was sitting at Jamie's bedside … again. Another CT scan had been run and they were waiting for a neurologist to look at it. More X-rays had been taken to check Jamie's broken ribs and the gash above his eye had been stitched this time instead of just closed with steri-strips.

"Can we go?" Jamie asked. His voice was thick with the sedative he'd been given. After he'd arrived at the hospital, all the touches from the ER staff had taken him from semi-conscious and confused right back to combative hysteria. Brayden had ended up wrapping both arms around Jamie and holding him tightly until one of the doctors had drugged him. To say it was a less than ideal situation was a gross understatement, but Brayden was so concerned about the seizure and further damage to other parts of Jamie's body it seemed like the only alternative.

"The neurologist hasn't gotten back to us about the CT scan yet, and I think they're considering admitting you," Brayden explained. He stroked Jamie's fingers. "I'm not sure I disagree with them. You had a seizure."

"Couldn't stop…"

"You couldn't stop what? Wigging out when they cuffed you? Believe me, I understand. That cop is a fucking idiot."

"Yeah that … but the jerking part too."

"You remember the seizure?" Brayden asked.

"Sort of … bits… it's foggy."

"Wow, that's weird, I thought people never remembered seizures because the brain was short-circuiting."

"I dunno." Jamie hugged Brayden's hand to his chest.

***

The ER doctor finally decided to admit Jamie to hospital. The primary reason seemed to be that no one could agree on whether the CT scan actually showed any reason for the seizure. Brayden made a brief trip down to the cafeteria to get a soda and then returned to the room Jamie was assigned.

In the hallway outside the room, Brayden was stunned to see his older brother Steve.

"Hello, Bray'." Steve Milbourne wore a well-tailored dark suit and pale blue shirt.

"Steve, what the hell are you doing here?"

"I came to find Jamie Ketelsen."

Brayden was baffled. "How do you know him?"

47

"Technically speaking, he works for me. Can we talk about this inside the room?" There was another man standing behind Steve, a shorter man with dark, collar-length hair. "This is Nick Diorides. He works for me too," Steve explained. "Nick, stay out here and keep an eye on the door. Nobody but us gets in."

Nick nodded.

Brayden gestured with his hand to the door and followed his brother inside. Steve Milbourne worked for a shadowy, covert government agency known as Division P. The obsessively secretive organization recruited psychics, primarily from other government jobs, trained them and then loaned them out on an as-needed basis to other agencies. Steve had tried to recruit Brayden, more than once. Brayden's refusal was a point of contention between the two of them.

Shutting the door, Brayden turned to face Steve. "Okay, start explaining."

"Is he okay?" asked Steve.

"Somebody tortured the crap out of him. He's suspected of murder. He had a seizure, and he's in the hospital. What do you think? Start talking, Steven, because there are obviously things you know that I don't."

"A little over a week ago, Ketelsen dropped off the CIA's radar. He wasn't running an active op, and nobody at the CIA paid much attention until he missed a check-in about three days later. They tried to get in contact with him. No luck. Because Division P sometimes borrows Jamie for other assignments, they contacted me. Ketelsen is on my roster. We've used him on several west coast assignments. He wasn't on a job for "P", but I used my less traditional resources to trace him here. Your turn. Go back to the part about tortured," Steve said.

"As far as we can tell, someone abducted him, beat the shit out of him, and either he escaped or was dumped."

"Why didn't he get in touch with his CIA handlers? They have a support network." Steve looked puzzled.

"Because his memory is trashed."

"He doesn't remember who took him?" Steve asked.

"He didn't remember his own name," Brayden replied.

Steve raised an eyebrow.

Brayden continued. "He can't read or write. He can't tie his shoes and he can't tell time. There are some serious neurological issues going on and he's barely holding it together. Today, my captain insisted he be questioned regarding a body that was found in the James River. One of the uniformed cops got rough and things went to hell really fast."

"Um, okay…Why is he with you?"

"I'm the one who found him. We're friends. We met a couple of months ago."

"Friends?" Steve asked.

"Fuck-buddies. Lovers. Whatever the hell you want label it," Brayden snapped.

"Bray', you know I have no problem with your sexual choices. I was just trying to get a feel for how well you know him."

There was a small sound from the bed. Brayden looked back to see Jamie sitting up, looking sleepy and confused.

"It's okay. This is somebody I know." Brayden pointed at his brother. "Do you remember working for Division P?"

Jamie frowned. "No."

"Brayden was just telling me about your memory problems. I'm Steve Milbourne, Brayden's brother. I manage the west coast operations for Division P. You've worked for me intermittently for about four years."

"Doing what?" Jamie asked.

"Intelligence work. We recruit primarily from the military and the other federal agencies, psychically train our people, and then return them to their regular jobs. Later, we periodically recall them and send them out on other assignments."

"And I'm one of your psychics?"

"Yes. You have mid-level telepathic skills. Have your psi senses been damaged along with the other problems that Brayden was telling me about?"

"I have no idea. Why exactly are you here?" Jamie squinted up at the two other men.

"You went missing and the CIA had no idea where you were. Nick's one of our finders. He helped me locate you," said Steve, pointing a thumb back toward the closed door.

Jamie rubbed his hand down over his face then looked up at Brayden.

"He's telling you the truth," said Brayden. "Or at least as much as he knows."

Jamie nodded and looked like he was trying to digest the information.

"Do you mind if I have look inside your head?" Steve asked. "People with psi talents process trauma different than rest of the population. There might be something simple and obvious to me that would help you with the rest of the problems Brayden said you've been having."

"Is that a good idea? I mean he had a seizure about five hours ago," said Brayden.

"I just want a peek. I'm not going to do anything."

The expression on Jamie's face was resigned and frustrated. "It's okay. Nothing seems to be helping much with my memory problems, and the doctors have no idea why I had the seizure."

Steve sat on the bed beside Jamie and touched a couple of fingertips to Jamie's temple. There was a long moment of stillness between Steve and Jamie. Jamie's eyes fell closed. Brayden watched all the blood drain out of Steve's face and his brother suddenly tipped sideways and nearly fell off the edge of the bed. Jamie's face was screwed up in pain.

"Steve? Jamie?" Brayden said. He wasn't sure which one he was more worried about.

"Holy fucking hell…" muttered Steve. He blinked hard before he stared up at Brayden. "I'm surprised he's not in a coma. I've never seen damage like that."

"Yeah, is it any wonder that he has amnesia issues along with all the other stuff?" Brayden said. Steve stood up and walked across the room, obviously contemplating his observations. Brayden took Steve's place sitting on the bedside. "Are you okay?" He curled a hand against Jamie's neck.

"Sorta," Jamie whispered.

Brayden rubbed his thumb gently across Jamie's skin, hoping the touch soothed him. It must have been welcome because Jamie leaned forward and rested his head on Brayden's shoulder.

Steve came back to face them. "Division P's headquarters are only about two hours from here. They have a healer and a really good clinical psychologist. Both of them are psi themselves and specialize in working with other psi. I have my own team in L.A., but headquarters is a whole lot closer. I think I should take the two of you there first thing tomorrow morning," said Steve.

"I have a job, and several active cases, and I'd really like to keep tabs on what happened to Jamie," said Brayden.

"I'll arrange for a few days leave of absence for you," replied Steve.

"I don't think…" Brayden began.

"Division P has federal jurisdiction. We fall loosely under Homeland Security. If I can't wrangle a few days off for you to accompany Jamie to Suffolk, the director can."

"Uh… why take me? Not that I'm complaining, it's just Jamie's the one who's injured."

"Bray' you're not headblind; you know having other psi around is important when there's a crisis. Although he and I know each other, he's not remembering that currently; that makes you even more important." Steve rested a fist lightly on top of Brayden's head. "If the two of you have a thing, he needs that now. Brayden, look at him. I'm almost willing to bet you're the only person he's voluntarily let touch him since this happened."

Brayden nodded slightly.

"I'm going to go make some phone calls. Nick is going to stay by the door. Nobody gets in until we have a game plan, and that includes hospital personnel. They're just keeping Jamie for observation, right?" Steve asked.

"As far as I know," Brayden answered. "Although there has been a mention of more testing."

"For now, I want nobody in here with him but you. If there's a problem, if he has another seizure or something, open the door and tell Nick."

"What aren't you telling me?" Brayden asked.

"Nothing that concerns you directly."

"Steve…"

"Just trust me for a little while. I'll get around to the messy jurisdictional details later."

Here comes trouble. Steve Milbourne stood at the far end of the hospital hallway, talking on the phone to Division P's director, Andrew Bottman. "Yeah, I know. The sooner we get a security and medevac team put together the better things like this will go… No, he seems to be stable. I'll call the complex when we get ready to leave. Bye."

Steve watched a man with jet-black hair approach the door where Nick was stationed. The two men had words and Nick gestured up the hallway at Steve. *Uh-huh, now we get to see whose is bigger.* The dark haired man stalked up the hallway. Steve had met Marcus Steele, Jamie's CIA handler, a couple of times before.

"Milbourne, I want to know exactly why you think you can prevent me from debriefing Agent Ketelsen." Steele radiated annoyance.

"He wouldn't be able to stand up to that kind of interrogation," Steve replied.

"My agent, my call."

"No, actually, he wasn't on assignment for you. Have you forgotten the phone conversation where you demanded to know where I'd sent him?" Steve pointed out.

"It was a reasonable assumption. Now, I want to talk to him. All I've gotten is partial information saying he's a suspect in a murder investigation and now he's in the hospital. I want to hear the facts from Ketelsen."

"That might be quite a bit harder than you think." Steve gave Steele the condensed version, very sketchy on the psi injury part.

"Jesus fucking hell…" muttered Steele. "Was the seizure connected to the memory loss thing?"

"I don't know, but I suspect the medical people at Division P will be able to tell more about the situation."

"I wish I knew if this … thing that happened to him was connected to the ops he's been doing for The Company."

"I'm sure he does too. In the morning, I'm going to have him transported to HQ in Suffolk as long as the hospital confirms he can tolerate a couple of hours of riding in a car," said Steve.

"I want a report as soon as you know anything. In the meantime, I'm going to get some answers about this murder charge thing from the Richmond PD." Steele started to turn away, then stopped and turned back. "You'd better keep me in the loop, Milbourne."

Steve merely nodded.

***

Getting through security at Division P headquarters in Suffolk, Virginia was pretty epic. Braydon watched as the machine took a thumbprint scan in addition to an ID produced by Steve Milbourne. Brayden sat beside Jamie in the back seat of the rental car. Nick sat up front with Steve. They were told where to park and ushered into one of the complex's buildings to meet a man named Danny Valentine.

"Steve! Damn it's been a while since I actually saw you in person." The tall, blond-haired man shook Steve's hand.

"Yeah, you'd think as much time as you and I spend flying around the country, we'd cross paths more often. Danny, this is my brother Brayden. He's a detective with the Richmond PD. He's a friend of Jamie's, and I'm hoping he can help fill in some of the gaps while we sort this out."

Brayden shook hands with Valentine. "Nice to meet you."

Then Steve introduced Jamie.

"Have we met?" Jamie asked as he shook hands with Valentine.

"A couple of times. You went through the usual training protocol, but we don't know each other very well. All your Division P assignments after training have come through Steve." Danny cast a long, appraising look at Jamie. "Step one is addressing your physical injuries, Jamie." Then he glanced at Steve. "If you and Nick want to go grab some food in the cafeteria, I'll catch up to you shortly. In the meantime, I want Peter to have a good long look at Jamie before we involve Benford."

"That sounds like an excellent idea," Steve agreed.

Brayden felt a little left in the dark. "Um, what am I supposed to do?"

Danny touched a hand to Brayden's shoulder. "I'm expecting you to stay with Jamie. If his memory issues are as profound as Steve implied, he needs the one person he knows and trusts with him. I don't know how much Steve has explained the routines around here, but we very heavily encourage positive emotional attachments."

Lifting an eyebrow, Brayden studied Valentine for a moment. Everything in his Talents told him what Valentine said should be taken at face value. Okay, he'd play along.

***

Jamie followed Danny Valentine into the clinic. Brayden was close behind. The Division P clinic looked half like an ER, half like an office. The huge main room had four cubicles along the right hand wall, separated from each other by soft retractable dividers. The left-hand side was lined with desks and file cabinets.

A wiry man with sandy brown hair stood up from one of the desk and came to meet them.

"Jamie, this is Peter Vithoulkas. He's the healer in charge of Division P's medical team. I think the two of you may have met back during your training but I'm not certain," said Danny. "He's been given as much information about your situation and injuries as we know."

Jamie forced himself to hold out his hand and was relieved that shaking hands with Vithoulkas didn't give him the creepy abrasive sensation that being touched by the most of the hospital's people gave him.

"At the very least I know I can fix your physical injuries," said Peter. "And you are?" He turned to face Brayden.

"Brayden Milbourne. I'm a friend of Jamie's."

"And Steve Milbourne's brother," Danny added.

"Ah, I think I've heard Steve mention you," Peter said.

"I'll leave you to Peter then," Danny said and departed.

"Come on over and let me have a look at the damage." Peter gestured toward one of the hospital beds.

Jamie wasn't wildly thrilled about another medical exam, but he understood its necessity. He crossed the room and sat on the bed.

"Brayden, you can pull up a seat," Peter said. There was a stool against the back wall of the cubicle. Brayden sat. Peter's hands touched lightly on Jamie's face, tracing the stitches above his eye. Jamie flinched, not from pain but from the warm, soothing buzz that accompanied Peter's touch. "Relax. Even if what I'm doing was likely to hurt, I could block the pain. You wouldn't feel it."

"You're psi too." Jamie said. The man had to be, because Jamie was slowly coming to understand what a difference it made in the way a touch felt.

Peter grinned. "Yeah, you could say that." His hands moved down Jamie's face to his neck, then to his chest. "Broken ribs too? Somebody did a number on you."

"Yeah, I wish I knew who," Jamie said. The warmth flooding his body was making him acutely aware of his exhaustion.

"Do you want to lie down? This is actually going to take a while," Peter said.

Jamie shook his head slightly. Although rationally he knew he was safe, at the moment this was just one more unfamiliar place.

Peter crooked a finger at Brayden. "Scoot your stool over here." Brayden complied. Peter took Brayden's hand and placed it on Jamie's arm. "Better?" he asked Jamie.

Jamie nodded.

"Let's try this again. I want you to lie down. It's going to take me an hour or so to heal you. It won't be a complete job, but I should be able to get rid of most of the bruises and scrapes, and cut down on the pain from the broken bones," Peter explained. "I'm not trying to make you uncomfortable. Brayden can stay here right beside you the whole time."

***

Brayden watched Peter's face as the healer sat on another stool, slowly moving his hands along Jamie's body. It was a litany of small expressions, concern, surprise, and sadness. Jamie eventually relaxed enough that Brayden could tell he'd fallen asleep.

"I'm done for the moment," Peter said softly. "He's going to need a protein and calcium supplement to replace a lot of the nutrients I forced his body to cannibalize, but that can wait an hour or two."

"How's the ... damage in his head?"

Peter grimaced a little. "It's serious. I didn't do more than a cursory assessment of it. I need to consult with our staff psychologist before we do anything to try and heal that."

Brayden let himself sigh. He knew from his brother that Division P had some of the best available medical care, and he had hoped for a more positive answer from the man who had erased the bruises from Jamie's body as if by magic.

Peter reached out and laid a hand on Brayden's shoulder. "He's strong and reasonably healthy despite the beating he took. We'll figure something out. It's just going to take a little time. I'm going to go call Trevor, one of our other healers, to come to the clinic while I go grab some food. If you're hungry, the cafeteria is down the hall and hang a left; otherwise you're welcome to stay here with Jamie."

"I think I should stay. If he wakes up and doesn't see anyone he recognizes…"

"I understand." Peter stood up to go. "You're equally welcome to lie down beside him and hold him."

That suggestion was a little jarring after the two hospital trips where Brayden's presence was only tolerated due to being a police officer and his ability to keep Jamie somewhat calm. He wondered just exactly how much Steve had passed along about his personal life. At work, he was pretty damn close to being in the closet. To the best of his knowledge, only a couple of co-workers knew, and they were good at keeping their mouths shut. Of course after the events of the past couple of days, there might be some pointed speculation headed his way. Steve had always told him that Division P was completely open to all combinations of relationships, but Brayden had taken that as a "we won't fire you for being gay" policy. Peter's comment sure made it sound even more aggressively proactive than that.

***

An hour passed as Jamie slept on the hospital bed. Brayden was starting to feel like he'd spent huge chunks of the past few days in almost the same position, watching Jamie and worrying. Maybe it would get better soon.

Jamie stretched slightly and opened his eyes. Immediately, it was apparent he was looking for Brayden. Brayden stood up and touched a hand to Jamie's shoulder. Jamie relaxed somewhat.

"I swear every time I wake up it's someplace different," muttered Jamie.

"I know, but I think maybe you're in the right place now."

Across the room, a light-skinned black man sat at a desk typing on a computer. He stood up and walked across the room. "Hi, I'm Trevor Phillips. I'm one of the healers on Peter's team. How're you feeling?"

"Better, less stiff and achy," said Jamie.

"Good. If you're feeling up to it, I'm supposed to take you to talk to Danny Valentine. The sooner we can get a handle on what happened to you the better. Is that okay with you?"

Jamie cast a look at Brayden. Brayden nodded. Jamie took a deep breath and let it out slowly. "Answers would be good."

***

In a conference room, Danny handed a file folder to Jamie. It held at least a dozen sheets of paper as well as an obligatory personnel photo. Jamie flipped through the pages for about ten seconds, hoping something would suddenly gel and he'd be able to read it. It might as well have been written in ancient Greek.

Jamie handed the folder back to Danny. "I can't read it," he said.

"Damn, I forgot about that part," Danny replied and looked embarrassed. "Okay then, I'll read it to you, and you interrupt me at any time with questions."

A decision had been made by the Division P to tell him as many details about his life and multiple jobs as they knew, in the hopes of jogging his missing memory. It did help a little. Jamie found a few, dim, fragmented memories of college, being in a street market in Syria, and doing small arms quals on a shooting range, but not much else.

"Even if you don't get it all back, I'm hoping you'll recover a fair amount if you give the whole situation a little time," said Danny. "All of our resources are at your disposal to help you. Anything you need, tell me, or Peter or anyone on staff. The next person you need to see is our staff psychologist."

***

"Come in, sit anywhere you like," said Dr. Stephen Benford as he beckoned Jamie into his office.

Jamie cast a brief, analytical glance at the psychologist as he walked into the room. The man was dark-haired, medium height, and in his mid to late forties. Jamie thought he looked like he should be the head of an accounting department.

Settling in a big, tan upholstered chair, Jamie watched the man as he read something on a tablet computer. The room resembled a den more than an office. It held two chairs and a sofa as well as a messy desk stacked with books and folders.

Benford sat on the sofa. "How did your session with Peter Vithoulkas go?"

"Good. I … don't hurt anywhere near as much now."

"Excellent. Now, a stickier question. How are you feeling emotionally?"

"Um… rattled, not very well put together," Jamie guiltily admitted. "I keep freaking out like some little kid…"

"It's okay, don't be embarrassed. Loss of emotional control is a common symptom of neurological damage. I know most people don't associate the two, but it can come out as raging anger or uncontrollable tears or even lack of concern for normal events. It's probably going to take days or weeks or possibly even longer for you to regain some sort of equilibrium."

"Fabulous."

"We'll work on it. How 'bout we switch topics? I'd like you to tell me about the events of the past few days. Start with the first thing you remember."

Jamie began with his foggy memory of stumbling down the road in the dark. He rambled on for several minutes trying to stick mostly just to the facts.

Benford finally cut him off when the time line reached leaving the hospital that morning. "That's fine. I don't need to know the details of coming here or meeting Peter. The next thing I do need is to have a look at the inside of your mind. I will be as delicate and gentle as possible but it may not be comfortable."

Jamie swallowed hard and nodded.

Benford crossed the small space separating the sofa and the chair, and sat on the arm of the chair beside Jamie. He laid a hand on Jamie's shoulder, a couple of fingers touching the bare skin of Jamie's neck. "Try to relax as much as you can."

Jamie could feel the brush of Benford's presence against his own. It was searching and seeking. He forced himself to hold still despite a strong desire to pull away. Suddenly there was a pressure sensation and he plunged into an abyss of pain. It felt like red hot claws were dragging through his brain. Jamie lashed out in self defense.

***

"Open your eyes for me, Jamie. Come on, I know you can do it," said a familiar voice.

Jamie opened leaden eyelids and saw Brayden's concerned face above him.

"Hey." Brayden stroked the side of Jamie's face gently.

Jamie slowly realized he was lying on the floor of Benford's office, and there were several other people in the room. Peter Vithoulkas had a hand on Jamie's chest. Over on the sofa, Benford sat with a blood-spattered shirt and the other healer –

what was his name?--was kneeling in front of him, holding a wad of gauze to Benford's nose.

"Will you hold still, Stephen? I'm trying to make sure it's not broken," the other healer said. Jamie finally remembered the man's name was Trevor.

"Okay, okay, I'm fine. It's just a bloody nose," groused Benford.

"Then let me make sure it stops bleeding," replied Trevor.

Jamie blinked. Had he done that? Hit the psychologist?

"Jamie?" said Peter. "Are you back with us?"

"Yeah…" Jamie replied. "What happened?"

"You reacted violently to my heavy-handed stupidity," replied Benford. "However, I now know exactly what was done to you, even if I don't know who or why."

"Stephen…?" Peter said, looking at the man with puzzlement.

"Somebody, specifically a mental dominant like me, used his abilities to tear information out of Jamie's mind. It left some neurological damage in its wake. I poked a little too aggressively at one of the damaged sites and I suspect that simulated the original injuries a little too closely. Jamie defended himself in the only way he knew how, physically. We had kind of a scuffle then he lost consciousness. That's when I called you."

"Jesus…" muttered Peter. "Did he have another seizure?"

"No," Benford said. "As far as I can tell, he just simply passed out. I think he tripped a few too many circuits so to speak, but with everything that's happened, I wanted you to check him out."

"He's stable, though he could probably do with some really low-key downtime until tomorrow at least," said Peter. He and Brayden helped Jamie sit up.

"I'm glad he's okay," Benford said and poked at his nose. "You and I, and probably Danny and Steve Milbourne as well, need to have a serious discussion about a game plan. We also need to discuss the implications that there's somebody out there doing this kind of thing to our people on purpose."

***

It looked like a nice, upscale hotel room to Brayden. After the unsettling episode with the staff psychologist, Jamie and Brayden were taken to the residential wing of the complex by Peter. Nobody had even asked whether they needed one room or two. Brayden couldn't decide if his relationship with Jamie was that damn obvious or if this was an eerie side effect of an entire organization staffed by psychics.

"The cafeteria is open until midnight. You're free to take food, utensils, and whatever you need from there. They open again at six a.m. I live two floors up. If either of you has a problem during the night, just dial the operator. We'll all get together for breakfast at nine to discuss options. Any questions?" asked Peter.

Brayden glanced back into the room. Jamie had stretched out on the bed. "How long are you keeping him here?"

"At least three or four days, then we'll reevaluate. He's probably going to need occupational therapy to work on some of the neurological deficits."

"Like learning to read again?"

"Yes. Anything else?" Peter asked.

"I don't think so."

"I have a parting word of advice. Jamie may be stable at the moment, but he's also half an inch from coming unglued. He could really benefit from some skin time with you."

Brayden raised an eyebrow. Vithoulkas wasn't really telling him to get naked with Jamie, was he?

"Hold his hand, kick back, and cuddle while the two of you watch TV, or do the horizontal bop, your choice, just touch him. He needs it. See you tomorrow." Peter walked down the corridor.

Brayden stood frozen in the doorway. Since when did "make out" become a prescription? He shut the door slowly, walked back to the far side of the room, and sat on the bed beside Jamie. He could tell the man wasn't asleep. There was far too much tension in his body.

"Are you hungry?" Brayden asked.

"No," Jamie mumbled.

"Benford's okay. He's just a little banged up."

"I don't even remember hitting him. What the fuck is wrong with me?"

"Babe, it wasn't really any more than a reflex to the pain," Brayden tried to reassure him.

"It… " Jamie stopped.

"It what?"

"It felt an awful lot like …him."

"The guy who tortured you in the first place?"

"Yeah." Jamie plucked at the fabric of the bedspread.

"Benford did say he understood what had been done."

"I guess that's a step in the right direction."

Brayden stood up and crawled across Jamie to lie in the middle of the bed. He pulled Jamie into his arms and kissed him softly. Maybe Peter had a point. It did feel like Jamie was hanging a little too close to the emotional edge.

"Why don't we find something on TV and just veg?" Brayden suggested. He sat up and pulled off his polo shirt, dropping it on the floor. There was a remote on the nightstand and a flat screen TV hanging on the wall at the foot of the bed. He thumbed the remote until the channel displayed a football game. "College football?"

"That'll do."

Brayden stuffed the pillows tighter against the headboard and he leaned back on them, holding out an arm to Jamie. Jamie scooted up to lay his head on Brayden's chest. Brayden could feel the prickle of Jamie's stubble on his skin.

"How 'bout we ditch your shirt too?"

It went in the same direction as Brayden's. The game was kind of lame, one team was basically slaughtering the other. Brayden let his gaze rove over Jamie's naked torso. The bruises had faded all the way to yellow smudges and the scrapes were just pink skin. Damn, the healer had done a pretty awesome job on the visible damage. Brayden remembered Peter saying that the cracked bones would only be partially healed, however. He rubbed his hand on Jamie's back, trying to get tight muscles to relax more.

Jamie tipped his face up toward Brayden's. He was silent, but Brayden felt a screaming undercurrent of tension still running through him. Brayden kissed him slowly, nipping at Jamie's lower lip, tracing the corner of Jamie's mouth with his tongue. Jamie's lips parted against his and Brayden explored the depths of his lover's mouth. He could feel Jamie unwinding a fraction, the angry self-doubting anger easing.

They were pressed lightly together from shoulder to thigh, naked from the waist up. Brayden cupped a hand against the back of Jamie's head and kissed his way along the rough length of Jamie's jaw to his ear and then down the side of his neck. It wasn't meant to be a seduction… honest.

Want to be in you, Jamie murmured inside Brayden's head. It was a raw, needy emotion from a man who obviously felt like he was spiraling out of control.

Brayden swallowed hard. He knew precisely what Jamie was asking. He'd bottomed exactly once before in his life. It hadn't been unpleasant; it just hadn't been amazing either. The wild weekend he'd spent with Jamie months ago had involved Jamie being a pushy, aggressive bottom who knew exactly what he wanted. This… Brayden realized was a request for trust.

"We don't have any lube or anything…" Brayden said.

"The bathroom's around here seem to be pretty well stocked."

"Okay, maybe there's hand lotion." Bareback was risky but Brayden wasn't sure he actually cared.

Jamie slid off the bed and vanished into the bathroom. The sounds of cabinets and drawers opening and shutting could be heard. Jamie returned, with items in his hand. He laid a bottle of slick and a pack of condoms on the bed. "Either somebody left these behind or someone believes in preparing for all eventualities."

"Should I be wowed or creeped out?"

"I don't know." Jamie took off his jeans and deposited them on top of the discarded shirts.

Brayden slowly rolled off the bed and stripped the rest of the way. He stood looking down into Jamie's eyes, so blue, so vulnerable. He'd seen Jamie absolutely hysterical enough times in the past few days to know that even the calm moments were closer to a breakdown than they should be. Sex wasn't a solution… was it? That healer seemed to think there was something to it. Steve had hinted at deep connections between psi on more than one occasion. It wasn't like he and Jamie hadn't done it before… but it was the fact that Jamie didn't remember that bothered Brayden.

Jamie cupped his hands around Brayden's face. "I need you so bad. We've gotten close a couple of times. I trust you. I need you to trust me."

Brayden kissed him, letting all his psychic shielding fall away.

Jamie's mouth opened against his and together they sank back onto the bed, sloppy misaimed kisses as they tried to stretch out without losing physical contact with each other. Brayden was already mostly hard when Jamie began to fondle his balls. They'd spent so much time kissing and touching. Jamie nipped at one of Brayden's nipples.

"Damn, go easy." Brayden writhed under Jamie.

Jamie chuckled. "Sensitive there?"

"Yeah, kinda."

Jamie licked Brayden's nipple instead. "Better?" His fingertip circled Brayden's anus.

"Just get on with it and stop torturing me," Brayden said.

It took Jamie a moment to deal with the bottle of lube, then cool wetness was pushing in. Reflex took over and for a moment Brayden's body trying to reject the intrusion.

"You okay?" Jamie asked softly.

Brayden could sense his hesitant concern. "Yeah. I just…" He didn't have a good excuse.

"I'll go slow."

Brayden took a deep breath and blew it out. Jamie placed a line of kisses down Brayden's belly. There was a lot of emotion there. The slight discomfort turned into pleasure as Jamie's finger slipped against Brayden's prostate. Brayden groaned.

Better?

Brayden nodded. Jamie's tongue dragged down the length of Brayden's cock and back up. Oh God that was good. Jamie's timing was impeccable, because that had to have been more than one finger pushing in as Jamie's mouth sucked on the tip of Brayden's cock. Two? Three? There was a bit of a burn but the stroke hit exactly the right spot.

"Just… there…God… more…" Brayden couldn't get his mouth to cooperate.

Jamie paused for a minute to roll on a condom. Brayden's leg was hooked over Jamie's shoulder, and he could see the intensity in Jamie's eyes. The pressure was different. Jamie's dick wasn't huge, but it wasn't tiny either, and it felt a hell of a lot bigger than a couple of fingers. Brayden gulped. Jamie's hand stroked Brayden's cock. Inside, outside, the whole sensation was overwhelming Brayden, he could feel himself edging close to blowing. He grabbed his dick and squeezed, trying to delay the climax. It worked, a little, until Jamie began to thrust into him.

Pulse pounding, fingers clenching in the sheets, Brayden could feel Jamie in his body and in his head. The explosion hit with volcanic force. Vision graying, his dick pulsed streams of come up his belly as muscles clenched and electricity shot through his nervous system. Just beneath the surface, he could feel Jamie's orgasm ripping through like an echo.

Jamie sprawled on top of Brayden, their bodies practically sealed together with sweat and semen. The connection between their minds was a heated swirl of pleasure and fatigue.

Chapter 5

"The idea that there's someone with your skill set out there that lacks your ethics is really kind of disturbing," said Danny, meeting Stephen Benford's gaze. They sat in Danny's office. The rest of the complex was very quiet this late in the evening.

"What's that old adage, 'with great power, comes great responsibility'? It sickens me that someone would make use of those Talents in such a way," replied Stephen.

"It's not like we operate under the illusion that there aren't some very sick individuals out there, but I had hoped we had the advantage when it came to training people to use those Talents."

"There's no guarantee the unsub has any formal training. Considering the brutal nature of the damage, he could have raw talent that he's learned to utilize through sheer trial and error," Stephen suggested.

"Great… that makes it sound so much better."

Stephen grinned slightly. "I'm just pointing out the possibilities."

"Do we view this as an active threat against our people or was the whole thing just incidental to Jamie being a Division P agent?"

"Based on a single known incident, I'm not sure there's any way to tell."

"I guess that also means we need to get every single one of our people to check in and make sure all are present and accounted for," Danny said. "I'll get Evy to start making phone calls today."

"Don't forget the CIA component to this. Jamie spends ninety percent of his time working for them, and we know there is some excruciatingly high risk to that."

"Steve Milbourne had a little tete-a-tete with Marcus Steele, Jamie's handler. Steele seems to be as much in the dark about why this happened as we are."

"What was the last op Jamie ran for the CIA?" Stephen asked.

"Something in Syria. I don't know any details. I think Milbourne was considering choking a little more information out of Steele."

***

Sunlight filtered dimly through a crack in the curtain, and Jamie glanced half asleep at the clock on the night stand. It displayed angular blocky lines that he comprehended had to be numbers. He just had no idea which ones. Rolling on his back, he stared at the ceiling in frustration. Beside him, Brayden made a low noise and opened one eye.

"Morning," Brayden mumbled. He slung an arm around Jamie's body and hauled him close.

Jamie snuggled against the familiar warmth of Brayden's body and a memory clicked into place. *Brayden was sprawled naked on his belly on the sofa. Jamie came back from the kitchen with a beer bottle in hand. The heavily muscled curve of Brayden's ass was just too good to resist. Jamie leaned over and lightly bit him.*

75

"You feel a little closer to … normal," whispered Brayden. He placed a kiss on Jamie's mouth and morning wood pressed solidly against Jamie's thigh. "What time is it?"

"I don't know. The sun is up." He felt sleepy puzzlement from Brayden followed by a slow comprehension of the problem.

"Give me your hand." Brayden took hold of Jamie's hand, folding the fingers to leave only the index finger up. He traced the numbers on the plastic face of the clock with Jamie's finger. "Seven one four, so that means it's seven-fourteen in the morning. Okay?"

"I feel like a five-year-old, except I don't remember being five."

Brayden let go of Jamie's hand and cupped his hands around Jamie's face. "Don't. It's only been three days. If the healer hadn't done his magic on your body, your bruises wouldn't even be fading yet. Go take a shower. We have some time before we have to go do the breakfast meeting."

It took only a few minutes for the shower to warm and Jamie stood under the water staring at the drain. The swirl of water going down the drain was perfectly clear, and he found it disturbing that he had even wondered if it would be otherwise.

***

The sound of his cell phone ringing stopped Brayden before he reached the bathroom. He fished it out of the jeans on the floor and answered it. "Milbourne."

"It's Sam. I have an update you probably don't want to hear," she said. "Some of the blood on Ketelsen's jeans matches the blood type of the car in the river vic," said Samantha.

"Which narrows it down how much?" Brayden asked, phone in hand, pacing the room.

"Down to about forty percent of the population. O positive is the most common."

"What about DNA?"

"You know that's going to take at least another week, but it may get taken completely out of my hands."

"Why?" Brayden asked.

"It seems the prime suspect, your buddy Ketelsen, works for the CIA. Did you know that?"

"Yes," Brayden said slowly.

"Rumor has it the CIA is leaning very heavily on the captain to turn the case over to DHS. I think that sucks. No offense, Milbourne, but if the guy murdered somebody, he ought to be held responsible," said the forensic tech.

"Sam, I'm not sure it's anywhere near that straightforward. Would you accuse a cop of murder if he killed someone in the line of duty?"

"Okay, I get your point. But amnesia? Really? Does Ketelsen really think he can pull that off?" Samantha asked.

"He has verifiable neurological damage, and he had a seizure in the precinct."

"Oh."

"Thanks for the information. I'll be in touch tomorrow," said Brayden.

"I won't be here. Tomorrow's Saturday and I actually don't have to work. Miracles do happen. I'll pass the word along that you want to have a look-see at the report though."

"Thank you and call me when you get back," Brayden replied.

"Yeah, okay."

Brayden tossed the phone onto the bed and walked into the bathroom.

Chapter 6

"The flat line at the top and the long curve that drops down from it makes it a letter 'J'," said Sumiko.

Jamie glances sideways at the woman in the wheelchair beside him. She had white-blond, shoulder length hair and a somewhat sharp, angular face. He'd been told by Danny Valentine that the focus for the morning was having a woman named Sumiko Pierce tutor him in some very basic reading and writing skills. She seemed nice, Jamie thought, and damn patient too, considering he was an adult who didn't recognize the letters of the alphabet.

"It's brain injury," she said softly. "You aren't stupid, you just have learn it again."

He heaved a sigh. "I know… I just feel… frustrated. I could tell you in exquisite detail how to field strip a Sig, but I can't read my own name."

"It'll come. I'm familiar with the frustration concept. It's taken me fourteen months to be able to walk a dozen steps on my own."

"Accident?" he asked.

"Yes. Miata versus Escalade. Bet you can guess which one I was in."

"Ow."

"I'm healing, slowly, but it's getting there. Let's go through the letter flash cards a couple more times, then call it quits. This is highly unlikely to be a quick fix."

***

When Brayden met Jamie in the cafeteria for lunch, he thought Jamie looked frazzled. They sat near a window to eat.

"So, what did you do while I was trying to figure out why the letters J and L look way too similar?" asked Jamie.

"Spent an hour talking to Steve. We swap email weekly, but we don't talk much. Then it was my turn in the hot seat with Dr. Benford."

"Why did he want to see you? It's not like you know anything about what happened to me."

"It had more to do with what I knew of your behavior patterns and all from before, and then it segued sideways into how I thought you were coping now." Brayden didn't include that Benford had tried to impress upon him the idea that Jamie needed his support very badly. As if Brayden hadn't already figured that out. It had gotten even weirder when Benford had made some rather specific suggestions about how physical Brayden should get with Jamie.

"I guess that falls somewhere in the category of standard psych-eval stuff. Sometime late this afternoon, they want me to get together with a forensic artist. Valentine said she specializes in getting useable descriptions of assailants from crime victims." Jamie ran a hand down over his face. "I guess I qualify."

80

Brayden reached across the table and laid a hand on Jamie's wrist. He could feel Jamie's pulse steady and even, but there was a significant layer of tension overlaying it. "Let's eat and go for a walk," he suggested.

"Okay, I guess."

It only took them another ten minutes or so to eat, then Brayden shepherded Jamie out the door into the cool air. They ended up following a long gravel path that wound its way along the perimeter of the complex grounds.

"How big do you think this place is?" asked Brayden.

"Mmm, maybe a hundred acres or so. It's kind of weird, but I like the way this place feels. It feels quiet."

"I wonder if they did something to make it feel that way."

"I guess maybe it's possible," said Jamie.

They were fairly far from the buildings and a certain amount of shrubbery and trees lined the path. Brayden took Jamie's hand. "I need to go back to Richmond tomorrow. I talked to one of the forensic techs and the blood from the jeans you were wearing matches the dead guy's."

"Just great," Jamie muttered bitterly. He stopped walking.

"It's circumstantial. There's no weapon, no crime scene and no witnesses. I'm still betting on self defense, given the injuries you had."

Jamie stared at the ground until Brayden tipped his face up with a finger. Tears brimmed in Jamie's eyes. "I am such a fucking wreck." He pulled away and started down the path again.

Brayden stood watching him go for a few seconds then went after him. "You didn't let me finish." He fell in step beside Jamie. "I'll only be gone for the day. Just long enough to get there, get some information, and get back. I'll be back by evening."

"Fine."

Taking Jamie's hand again, Brayden walked in silence, willing to let Jamie brood for the moment.

***

The forensic artist was evidently someone that didn't work at the Division P complex on a regular basis. Jamie was asked to wait in yet another room with a table and several chairs. This room however had a big glass mirror along one wall, and Jamie was savvy enough to suspect was one-way glass. Danny Valentine showed the woman into the room, and Jamie noted the hand Danny had on her shoulder. The woman walked with a heavy limp and her lower right arm was in a brace.

"Jamie, this is Jennifer Sebastiano. She's going to try and help us get some visual descriptions of the people who took you," Danny introduced her.

Jamie shook hands carefully, all the while taking a good look at her. She was barely average height, had a softly rounded body shape and brown hair in a single braid that hung down past her

82

waist. She had a sketch pad tucked under her arm and several pencils in her hand.

"Nice to meet you Jamie. I wish it was under better circumstances," she said.

Danny brushed his fingers along Jennifer's neck. "This one may be a little different than usual. Since he's one of ours, so all the information you get is potentially useful."

Jamie decided that Danny and Jennifer probably had a relationship. Nobody touched with that kind of careless affection it they were just colleagues.

"I'll core dump everything I get, then we can study it later," replied Jennifer.

Nodding slightly, Danny departed.

Jennifer settled in one of the chairs. "Let me tell you a little bit about what I do. Like Danny said, you're just a bit different than the usual people I work with. Under most circumstances, I give out very little information as to how I get such accurate descriptions. Since you are Division P, just like I am, I can be more up front with you."

"Is that better or worse?" Jamie asked.

"I guess we'll find out. Let's start with something fairly simple. The report says Detective Brayden Milbourne found you walking on a road. Think about the road, the color, the texture, if there are trees or houses."

Jamie did as he was told.

Jennifer moved on to ask him about his memories of being bound, telling him to focus on just his wrists at first. "What do you think they used to bind your wrists? Does it feel like plastic? Or tape?"

"Plastic. I th-think it was zip ties."

"Okay. Now look down, can you see your feet or your legs?"

"My legs. My ankles are tied to the chair legs."

"What's the floor look like?" she prompted.

Jamie dug in his fractured memory for the small detail. "Tile, grungy gray, probably vinyl tile." He also saw the tips of shoes.

"Now tell me about the person in front of you."

Jamie took a sharp breath. There was going to be pain. He'd already been hit several times. The man had a dusky brown skin tone, and heavy thick hair on his chest that showed in the gap at the top of his shirt. The expression on his face was a stony glare, and Jamie was suddenly uncertain if he was likely to survive.

"What do you know about the guidance system for the Hammerhead missile? Is the CIA aware there are plans on the market? There are rumors the CIA is placing a bid. Is this true?" the man demanded.

Jamie was silent. The man slammed a fist into Jamie's stomach. The pain was fairly intense, but it didn't compare to the pressure inside his head. It was pushing at his shielding with brutal force. A male hand wearing a ring came around the side of his face. The skin tone was much paler than the man in front of him.

Jamie tried to lean away but the hand gripped the side of his skull. The pressure escalated from simple pain to unbearable…

Jamie screamed.

***

If Brayden could have leapt straight through the one-way mirror to reach Jamie, it still wouldn't have been fast enough to suit him. He scrambled out of the neighboring room where he watched through the one way glass with Valentine. He yanked open the door of the room where Jamie was located. Danny Valentine was barely half a step behind him.

By the time Brayden reached Jamie, the man was lying on the floor, thrashing and clutching his head. Brayden dropped beside him and tried to pull Jamie up into his arms. He very nearly got a knee to the face for his efforts. He didn't want to restrain Jamie as he would a violent suspect, because he feared that would make the situation worse, so he settled for simply laying on top of Jamie. His heavier body weight pressed Jamie flat to the floor.

"Jamie. It's Brayden. Quit fighting me. You're safe, I promise." He tried to keep his voice as even as possible. Beneath him, Jamie slowly calmed, body motion dwindling to a few reflexive jerks. Finally Jamie lay still, breathing hard.

Brayden spared a glance toward Danny and Jennifer. Jennifer was madly sketching as Danny hovered inches away from her. Her face was pale and pinched. When she finished and laid her pad and pencil down, Danny reached out and drew her into his embrace.

Returning his focus to Jamie, Brayden lifted slightly, taking some of his weight off his lover. "Jamie, talk to me."

"Is he gone?" Jamie's voice was barely audible.

"He was never here. This is Division P. He can't reach you here." Brayden rose up on his hands and knees, and looked down into Jamie's face. Tears seeped slowly from Jamie's eyes. "Do you think you can sit up?"

Jamie nodded and let Brayden help him.

Scooting backward to lean against the wall, Brayden drew Jamie close so his butt sat between Brayden's thighs and Jamie's body leaned on his chest. One arm held Jamie snug against him, the other stroked Jamie's hair. Brayden glanced back toward Danny and Jennifer. "Please tell me you got something useful out of this. I swear this is worse than making a rape victim relive her attack."

"What makes you think it wasn't a rape?" asked Jennifer. Her voice sounded hollow and flat.

Brayden was shocked and confused. "He was examined at the hospital. There was no evidence of blood or tearing."

"A rape doesn't really have to be physical penetration," she said. "Rape is all about force, and lack of consent and intimate damage. Jamie's rape may not have been physical, but it was still rape." She stood slowly and walked out of the room.

Danny made a move as if to follow her then hesitated. He turned toward Brayden and Jamie, looking faintly embarrassed.

"She may have a point," said Brayden.

"She often has a point and is willing to smack you up beside the head with it too. I love her to death, but tact isn't always her strong suit," replied Danny. "Jamie, do you want me to call Peter to come have a look at you?"

"No." Jamie's voice was so soft Brayden doubted Danny could hear it.

"I'll take him back to the room we slept in," said Brayden. "If that's okay by you."

"Yes, that's probably a good idea. I'll swing by in a couple of hours and let you know what we gleaned from Jen's sketches. Listen I know this probably feels like we're subjecting Jamie to way too much, but given the circumstances we're pretty desperate to find out who did this too him and why."

"I'm a cop, remember? I get it, I really do. It's just doesn't make it any easier to watch him be put through it all again."

"I know. I really need to go check on Jennifer. She's amazing at what she does, but she pays a really high price in return. I suspect tonight will be really bad." Danny walked slowly out the door.

Brayden wondered about the "high price" and what exactly that meant. Damned if it didn't seem like more than half of all the benefits you got from being psi, had a serious down side.

***

Why oh why can't I get past this? Why do I keep freaking out? Jamie followed Brayden into the assigned room, and when Brayden sat on the wide sofa, Jamie willingly crawled into his lover's lap.

"I thought I was getting better at dealing with what happened," Jamie said.

Brayden rubbed Jamie's back and kissed him softly on the temple. "It hasn't even been a week. And the things Jennifer dredged up… were some of the worst memories."

"For a few minutes… I thought he was there… still there… there again. Bray', he made me hurt worse than getting shot, worse than breaking my ankle…Why do I suddenly remember breaking my ankle?" Jamie whispered. "And I still have no idea who he is."

"We'll figure it out."

"Don't lie to me, I'm not a child." Jamie snapped.

"Okay then, we'll all do our damnedest to try and figure it out."

Jamie heaved a sigh of near despair. "That I might believe."

***

The knock on the door was Danny. When Brayden opened it, Danny was standing in the hallway. The man had changed from his dress shirt and slacks into jeans and a tan T-shirt with USMC emblazoned across the front.

"How's he doing?" Danny asked.

"Better. He's stronger than you'd think."

"He has to be, to withstand what was done to him. Anyway, I went through the sketches with Jennifer. I'd like to discuss some of the information with the two of you, if you think he's up to it," Danny said.

Jamie slowly walked toward them. "I'll survive. The more we know, the closer we get."

"Why don't we all go down to the cafeteria and get some coffee and food if you like? There's not very many people left in the complex this late in the day."

Brayden glanced at Jamie for assent. Jamie nodded.

In the cafeteria, they all sat around a table as Danny began to pull sketches from the folder. The first few were fairly innocuous: a road and trees that might possibly be the road that Brayden lived on, knees not quite obscuring ankles zip tied to chair legs, a barren cinder block wall and battered institutional style desk. Then the images were more disturbing. A dark-skinned man with a blade of a nose and a hint of a delighted snarl on his face.

Jamie swallowed hard and looked away.

"We're currently running the sketch through facial recognition software in six different agency databases. Maybe we'll get a hit," said Danny.

"You still have one more sheet," noted Brayden.

"Yes, and possibly the most interesting of the lot in some ways."
Danny flipped over the last page. It showed a male hand with
thick blunt fingers and a wide heavy ring. The ring had a crest of
the top surface and some partially visible letters that might be D
and U. "This looks like it might be a university ring or possibly
related to armed forces in another country."

"He had an accent," Jamie blurted out. "He didn't speak very
much but his accent was … I would say Scandinavian maybe? It
wasn't quite guttural enough to be German."

Danny picked up a pencil and made a notation on the back of the
page. "I'll tell the tech people to focus on Interpol first."

***

Steve Milbourne and Brayden left early the following morning to
drive back to Richmond. As Steve pulled the car into Brayden's
driveway, Brayden's thoughts were on Jamie. He knew Jamie
was inherently safe at the Division P complex. After all, the
place rivaled a military base in its security, but still… he worried
about Jamie's ability to cope.

"He'll be okay. I promise," said Steve.

"You always could read me like a book," replied Brayden.

"Big brother privileges."

Brayden punched him lightly in the shoulder. "Ass."

"Are you going to talk to the department people about the case
against Jamie?"

"Yeah, specifically a forensic tech I know."

"I'd like to go with you. The more information I have, the more likely we can defuse the situation and get Jamie cleared." Steve climbed out of the car.

"Okay. Let's take my SUV. It's got stickers so I can park in the department lot. Oh, I just realized I left my police radio in the house." Brayden got out and started toward the house. Steve was a few steps behind him. "You can wait in the SUV for me if you want."

"Okay."

Brayden pointed his key ring in the general direction of the SUV and pushed the button to unlock it. It made the characteristic chirp, followed by a dull whump of pressure, then the SUV exploded.

Chapter 7

The force of the explosion blew Brayden off his feet and bowled him several feet across the lawn, knocking the breath out of him. Dazed, with ears ringing, he lay there for some unknown number of seconds gasping and trying to process. Boom. Explosion. My truck. Steve?

He staggered to his feet, the world around him hazed by smoke and whirling at a nauseating speed. He fell flat and lay there for another period of time before he made a second try. He got to his hands and knees and looked around. Steve lay near the big oak tree in the front yard, unmoving, resembling a carelessly flung toy.

Brayden stumbled toward him and fell to his knees beside Steve, automatically pressing fingers to Steve's throat for a pulse. It was there, rapid and faint. Steve groaned, one hand fisting in the grass.

"Steve? Talk to me! Are you okay?" Brayden demanded. He could sense a tight wash of pure pain from his brother.

Steve's face contorted in a grimace of agony. "Hurts… bad."

"Where?" Brayden ran his hands lightly down Steve's arms and legs. There were several small bleeding gashes from debris.

"My back."

Those two words scared Brayden. "Can you feel your legs?"

"Yeah." Steve replied with another sound of pain. "But kinda feels like they're half asleep."

Brayden swallowed hard. "Wiggle your feet for me. Just a little."

Steve complied, flexing his ankles somewhat.

"Do. Not. Move." He lay his hand flat on Steve's chest and fished his cell phone from his pocket, dialing 911. "This is Detective Brayden Milbourne. Somebody blew up my truck in front of my house. I need police, fire, and an ambulance. I have an adult male, thirty-six years old with a suspected spinal cord injury from the blast." He rattled off his address.

Steve gripped Brayden's wrist where it lay on his chest. "Hurts like fucking hell."

Brayden dropped the phone on the grass without turning it off and took Steve's hand in his. "Hang tight. Help's coming."

"Call Division P."

The thought that Jamie might be in danger jumped into his thoughts, but then he realized that calling Division P would serve other purposes. They had Peter Vithoulkas, the healer who did impossible things.

"Where's your phone?" Brayden asked.

"Right pocket."

With a small prayer that Steve's phone had survived too, Brayden pulled it out. The screen lit up. "Whose number do I look for? Peter?"

"No, call Danny Valentine," mumbled Steve.

Scrolling down through names, Brayden found Valentine and called.

"Hey Steve, what's up?" answered Valentine.

"This isn't Steve. It's Brayden. Somebody blew up my truck. Steve's hurt, possibly pretty bad. There might be spinal cord damage. We need help, specifically your healer."

"Where are you?" Danny's voice was tight.

"In front of my house at the moment. Fire and rescue are on the way."

"I'll send a team to you ASAP. Call me back as soon as you know which hospital they're taking him to. What about you? Are you okay?"

Brayden looked down his body. Like Steve, he had a number of small cuts from flying shrapnel, but he belatedly noticed blood was dripping from fingertips of the hand not holding the phone. A glance further up his arm showed a long deep gash that ran from near his elbow almost to his shoulder. Blood was seeping steadily.

"I'll survive," he said. "EMS should be here soon."

***

In the brand spanking new Division P ambulance, Danny stared out the front window in silence for several minutes. Steve Milbourne was a friend. He and Steve had trained together three years ago before they realized they were being groomed for section chief positions during an internal re-organization of

Division P. Danny was assigned to the east coast and Steve the west.

A hand touched his shoulder, and Danny felt the familiar presence of his lover Peter. Peter had reached through the gap between the front seats.

"He'll be okay," said Peter. "This is why we bought the ambulance and set up the trauma team. I'm not going to let anymore 'Isabelle Rea's' happen." He was referring to an agent they had lost a year before due to a mix of psi shock and serious injury.

"And if Steve was hundreds of miles away, instead of a couple hours drive?"

"That's why I'm pushing Bottman to buy us a helicopter, so we can set up a truly proper medevac unit. Think about the nightmare of getting to Jen in Baltimore when she was attacked."

"At least his brother is with him. That should help with the psi shock problem in the ER," said Danny.

 In recent years, Division P had become aware that psi Talented individuals often coped badly with serious physical trauma. This was especially true when that trauma led to too many medical personnel touching the injured victim. For lack of a better term, they'd taken to calling it psi shock, and it was characterized by wildly fluctuating vitals and often severely depressed neurological function. There was no method to predict how likely or how bad the response would be. The only reliable factor was that the shock was lessened if another psi was present, particularly if the victim had an emotional attachment with the other psi.

"Is Brayden injured too?" Peter asked.

"I'm not really sure. He sounded lucid and relatively calm given the situation. I doubt he escaped unscathed, but I'm hoping any damage is fairly minor."

"Should we have brought Jamie?" Peter said.

"No, absolutely not," Jonas Nightengale chimed in from the driver's seat. "If somebody has serious intentions of killing Steve and Brayden, Jamie would be at risk anyplace other than P's complex." Jonas was an ex-SEAL who had recently transferred from the traditional part-time role at Division P to a full-time position managing facets of Division P security.

"I think that's a valid point," replied Danny. "It's been less than a week since he was kidnapped and tortured. It's reasonable to assume those people want anybody connected to Jamie dead."

"Have you talked to Reed or Vaughn?" asked Peter.

"No. Reed usually volunteers anything he knows; Vaughn, not so much. He's new and unsure of himself and only halfway through his training. We're still not sure how much of his Talent runs toward the precog slant and how much is clairvoyance."

***

The pressure of the bandages wrapped around Brayden's bleeding arm made him grit his teeth as he sat on the back bumper of the ambulance. The EMT beside him was taking his

blood pressure as Brayden watched his colleague, Mike
Simmons, stride toward him.

"Jesus Brayden, what the hell happened?" Simmons asked.

"Somebody rigged a bomb to the door locking mechanism on my
car, I think."

"This has something to do with that guy Ketelsen doesn't it?"

"Probably," Brayden admitted.

"Who's the guy they're putting on the backboard?"

"My brother." Brayden's eyes traveled over to Steve. He was
being carefully strapped down, head held immobile while the
foam blocks were set on either side. Brayden could feel a trickle
of fear from Steve. He saw another EMT bend close to listen to
something Steve said. The EMT patted Steve carefully on the
shoulder.

"Hey, Ken, if you're done with him, can you send your patient
over this way? His brother is getting a little antsy," called the
EMT beside Steve.

"Two minutes, I want to check his breath sounds," replied Ken.
He pressed a stethoscope to Brayden's chest. "Take a couple of
deep breaths for me."

Brayden did so, and ended up coughing several times because of
it.

"I'm not hearing anything definitive, but they'll probably want to
do a chest X-ray at the hospital. You are going to need a whole
mess of stitches for your arm though."

"Yeah, I know. Can I go talk to Steve now?" Brayden asked.

"Okay. Try not to flex your arm. I'm afraid it may start bleeding again."

Standing up slowly, Brayden walked over to where Steve lay secured to the backboard. An IV was being started.

"My legs still feel kind of weird, half asleep or something," said Steve. His breathing was fast and shallow.

Brayden knelt down and laid a hand on Steve's leg. "Which leg am I touching?"

"Left."

"See, that's a good sign." Brayden looked at the EMT for confirmation and the man nodded. "Your Division P guys are on their way. Peter does amazing things." He took hold of Steve's hand and squeezed it. He could feel his brother's fear a whole lot more keenly when he did. "Look at me. Breathe slow, Stevie. In. Out. Just like when Dad had to dig broken glass out of your knees. Push the pain off to the side."

 "I was eleven, Bray."

"Yeah, so? Doesn't change the fact you were in pain and about to spaz because of all the blood."

Steve stuck his tongue out at Brayden and gave him a lopsided smile. Good. Brayden could sense his brother's level of panic dropping back a few notches. He squeezed Steve's hand again.

***

98

Brayden sat on the gurney waiting for a doctor to come back and stitch up his arm. His arm was now a steady, throbbing ache. While he waited, he worried. Steve had been taken off for X-rays and an MRI, that much Brayden had heard from the neighboring cubicle. How much spinal cord damage did Steve have? The fact Steve had some feeling in his legs and could wiggle his feet was a good sign, wasn't it? He also worried about Steve wigging out again from all the medical people who'd been touching him.

A man entered the cubicle. Brayden was expecting a doctor or nurse, instead it was his captain.

"You gonna be okay?"

"I think so sir."

"I want the whole damn story about Ketelsen and the CIA and the murder vic from the river," demanded Captain Dean.

Brayden gazed at him levelly. "I don't know the whole story. Chances are I only know a tiny bit more than you."

"Somebody tried to blow you up. You haven't been involved in any other cases in the past couple of months that would lead me to believe there's some run of the mill psycho out there targeting just you. But Ketelsen shows up and things start going sideways. As soon as we think we might have some evidence linking him more definitively to the vic, some unnamed batch of feds spirit him and you away for three days. Meanwhile, some CIA spook starts snooping around and announces to me that this whole case may have national security implications. When I ask for details, I'm told it's above my pay grade. They haven't yanked the evidence from the forensic people yet, or issued a cease and desist, but I wouldn't be surprised if it was headed my way. Is the man who was with you at the explosion scene CIA?"

"No, he's my brother."

The Captain looked vaguely puzzled. "He's the one who ferried you and Ketelsen away from the hospital isn't he? What part of the alphabet does he work for?"

"P."

"What?" The Captain looked really confused.

"Division P. That's all I'm allowed to tell you."

"Great. Just great." Dean rolled his eyes.

"Is the bomb squad checking out my house? I'm really hoping there's no surprises waiting for me there," Brayden said.

"Yeah. They've got the dogs and techs going over it as we speak. You know, on second thought maybe it is better if the feds take this on, 'cause God knows I don't have the manpower to deal with bombs and terrorists." Dean rubbed a hand down over his jaw.

"Who said anything about terrorists?" Brayden asked.

"Oh, I forgot you probably don't know we traced the car's registration and it goes back to a dummy corporation out of Dubai. Is this Division P thing going to make you disappear again?"

"Possibly." Brayden caught sight of four men in black coveralls in the hallway with a gurney. He recognized three of them:

Valentine, Vithoulkas, and Phillips. "Make that very probably," he corrected himself. Hell was going to freeze over before he let them take Steve away without him going along. He slid off the exam table and slowly started toward the door.

Trevor intercepted him in the doorway. "You look like shit, Milbourne, and you're not going anywhere until I check you out." he said. He placed one hand on Brayden's shoulder and the other on his side and guided him back to the exam table. He immediately began running his hands lightly over Brayden, checking him out.

"Steve's... worse," Bradyen said, his voice hitching.

The medic checked Brayden's pupil response. "Peter's gone to get him. He's in good hands. Try not to worry too much. Calling us was the best possible thing you could do for him. They haven't put any sutures in yet, have they?"

"No. I've only been here maybe half an hour."

"I'll take care of it and get you re-bandaged while Peter and Danny make sure Steve's stable enough to transport."

"Who are you?" Captain Dean demanded.

"Division P. We have federal jurisdiction. That's all you need to know," said Trevor. "Unless you really want to watch me put sutures in his arm, I suggest you leave."

***

Danny Valentine glanced at Jonas Nightengale, Division P's new chief of security. The man drove the ambulance from Richmond back toward Division P, eyes focused on the road.

"Did you use the thumb drive?" asked Danny.

"Yep, it took about sixty seconds for it to upload the scrubbing program."

"The hospital's already not too happy about us removing Steve and Brayden from their care. They're going to be doubly unhappy when they find out all records regarding the two of them have been deleted from the system," said Danny

"Tough. It's safer for our people this way. I'll get the tech people to hack in and double check the deletes later today."

***

When Brayden sank onto a bench in the Division P infirmary, he felt utterly drained. Across the room he could see Peter working on Steve. The healer had one hand slipped under Steve's back and the other on top of his belly. On the way back in the ambulance, Peter had spared a moment to assure Brayden that though the injury Steve had was serious, it was recoverable. There was a fracture to the L1 vertebrae and it had banged up the spinal cord just a little, but the cord was still intact and would heal, especially with some active help from Peter. Pain control, a clamshell back brace, and rest were in Steve's immediate future, followed by some careful rehab.

Head tilted back against the wall, Brayden closed his eyes and allowed his worry about Steve to relax to a lower level. A heavy weight settled across his thighs, and Brayden's eyes popped back open. Jamie was in his lap, straddling his legs, hands cupping Brayden's face. Jamie rested his forehead on Brayden's, breath ghosting across Brayden's mouth. Jamie was a tightly wound ball of tension and concern.

"I knew something was wrong. They told me your car got blown up and… and I was afraid you were dead," Jamie murmured.

"I got lucky."

Jamie's mouth sealed over his, a hard, hungry, desperate kiss. One of Jamie's hands curled around Brayden's neck, the other fisted in the bloodstained fabric of his shirt as Jamie pushed his tongue into Brayden's mouth. Brayden let himself drown in the familiar presence of his lover until a small sound wrenched his attention away.

Trevor was standing a few feet away with a smirk on his face. Brayden drew in a sharp breath of embarrassment. He still hadn't quite adjusted to the fact nobody around here seemed remotely surprised by his relationship with Jamie.

"Not that I haven't walked in on Peter and Danny more than once," said Trevor. "But if you're not much into the exhibitionist thing, you're welcome to go back to your quarters. I suspect you could really use some rest anyway."

Brayden cast a look across to where Steve still lay on the hospital bed, eyes closed as Peter worked on him.

"He'll be okay. Peter's probably going to be at it for another hour or so. If Steve wants you, you'll only be in the next wing," Trevor tried to reassure him.

After a long moment of hesitation, Brayden mumbled, "All right."

As Jamie led Brayden to the room they were assigned, Brayden walked beside him in silence. Had it really only been early this morning that he'd left this place? It felt like days.

Inside the room, Jamie pushed the door shut then pressed Brayden back against it. Despite his smaller body mass, he pinned Brayden flat to the door, lips on the pulse point of Brayden's throat. The emotions flowing from Jamie were a chaotic mix of fear, anger, and lust.

"I could have lost you," said Jamie. "I've lost so much and you've been the only thing holding me together. I need you so badly and those... those people would have killed you." He hit the wall beside them with a loosely clenched fist. "Jesus God... You could be dead."

"I'm okay."

Jamie tapped a finger on the heavy bandage covering Brayden's upper arm. "This qualifies as okay?"

"So the okay part is relative."

Jamie made a little growl. "I want to see the rest of you. There's blood all over your clothes. I'm assuming it's yours?"

"Yeah, probably. The broken vertebrae was Steve's only real injury, aside from some nicks from flying debris."

Jamie was already pulling Brayden's shirt loose from his jeans. He unbuttoned it and eased it back off Brayden's shoulders, dropping it on the floor. The jeans and boxer-briefs were pushed off together. Brayden toed off his sneakers. Jamie bent to help him take off his socks.

"Fuck… it looks like you got attacked by a tornado of razor blades," muttered Jamie.

Brayden glanced down. Everywhere he could see was a myriad of little nicks and scrapes, more on the same side as his gashed arm and less on the opposite side. The corner of the house had evidently provided only partial protection from the blast.

Grabbing Brayden by the wrist, Jamie dragged him toward the bed and pushed him down onto it. He began to run his hands over Brayden's skin, as if noting each and every mark on Brayden's body. Some touches stung slightly.

After allowing his lover to examine him head to toe, Brayden wrapped an arm around Jamie and rolled over on top of him.

"I'm okay. Really. There's nothing that won't heal. Even the eighteen stitches in my arm will eventually just be a scar." Brayden murmured against Jamie's cheek bone. God… the feel of Jamie's thin wiry form under him was bringing back the hint of arousal that had begun back in the infirmary.

Jamie's hand gripped Brayden's hair, face angling for a deep, open-mouth kiss.

That hint of desire was turning into full on want. As Brayden ground his hardening cock against Jamie's body, the fly of Jamie's jeans dragged uncomfortably across sensitive skin. "How come I'm naked and you're not?" he asked.

"Forgot," mumbled Jamie, his mouth more engaged in giving Brayden a tonsillectomy than anything else.

"Then we need to fix that." Brayden began pushing up Jamie's T-shirt. It took another couple of minutes to strip his lover, mostly because Jamie would hardly let go long enough to cooperate. Finally Jamie was naked too.

Brayden lay still feeling the throb of the injury to his arm. Trevor had supposedly done a little healing while he was putting stitches in, but Brayden wasn't exactly sure what that meant. He didn't really want to take off the bandage to check either. All the motions he'd done in the past few minutes were ramping up the pain.

"We can quit right here. I don't want to hurt you. Just lying here against you is fine," said Jamie, who lay curled tight to Brayden's side at this point.

"How 'bout we compromise? I lie here and you ride?" suggested Brayden. "You're still not really all the way healed either." He could still see discolored skin from all of Jamie's bruises, mostly faded down to yellow green at this point. Brayden wasn't sure if Jamie would go for that idea or not; they were still feeling their way back toward an easiness in their relationship.

Jamie gave him a long look. "Deal." He reached up and took hold of Brayden's jaw. "And if it hurts you too bad, I will know." He rocked his hips against Brayden and Brayden could feel the stiff poke of Jamie's cock along his lower belly.

****

Kissing Brayden softly on the mouth, Jamie reached down and wrapped his fingers around Brayden's prick. His lover wasn't quite all the way hard, and Jamie had a moment's worry that maybe sex was a bad idea right now. Brayden thrust shallowly into Jamie's grip and Jamie sensed the arousal level in Brayden ramping up again. Rough and aggressive was out. Now why did he think that? Jamie scoured his damaged memory. Intimacy with Brayden over the past week had been fairly gentle and caring, but before? Somewhere in the back, there lurked a memory of getting screwed stupid up over Brayden's Hayabusa and trying not to tip the damn bike over.

"Jamie?" Brayden murmured.

"I remember hanging over the seat of your bike…"

Brayden snickered. "Not one of our better plans. You really remember that?"

"A little." Jamie began to stroke him, enjoying the low moan it drew from Brayden. Sitting up, Jamie grabbed the lube and the condoms off the night stand and straddled Brayden's thighs, taking care not to jostle Brayden's body too much. He poured some lube into his hand and slicked in between his ass cheeks and inside.

"Are you going to be okay without any more prep than that?" Brayden asked.

"It'll be fine." Something deep and familiar stirred inside Jamie, and it felt normal and right. He did the honors, rolling the condom over Brayden's stiff prick. Every touch between them felt warm and intimate. For a moment, Jamie's mind had a flitter of panic. If he had lost Brayden…

"Hey, I'm right here," whispered Brayden.

Jamie leaned forward and kissed him, then rose up and reached behind himself to line Brayden up. Sinking onto his lover's cock with deliberate slowness, allowing his body to stretch enough to accommodate Brayden's girth, Jamie sat back. So full, treading that fine edge between pain and pleasure. Brayden's hands settled on Jamie's hips. As Jamie rose up, Brayden gasped a little, and not in a good way.

"Let go, don't use your arm," said Jamie.

"'Kay." Brayden's voice was tight, and Jamie hesitated. "Keep going," Brayden said.

Jamie sank back down, impaling himself on Brayden's prick. A tense wave of pain echoed from Brayden. "Okay, no more. This was a bad idea. I'm sorry."

"It'll be fine. I'm okay," Brayden objected as Jamie sat down on the bed beside Brayden's hip.

"No, you're not." He petted Brayden's half-wilted erection. "You're in too much pain."

"And you're hard as rock." Brayden dragged his thumb across the leaking tip of Jamie's cock.

"So how 'bout you just watch, and I'll solve my own problem?" suggested Jamie.

"Let me finger fuck you. One arm still works."

"Mmm, I could go for that."

Brayden pushed himself to sit up against the head board. Jamie knelt in front of Brayden, butt aimed toward him, and handed Brayden the bottle of lube. The feel of Brayden's fingers inside him didn't provide the same level of pressure but the compensation of fingertips hitting the sweet spot dead on made up for it. Jamie stroked himself as Brayden's fingers pistoned in and out, taking him close to coming in a couple of minutes.

Jamie groaned and jacked himself a little faster. "Oh fuck…" The climax washed through him and he spurted long ropes of come across the bed. He finally sank, belly down, onto the sheets, breathing hard. Brayden rubbed Jamie's lower back. Jamie finally twisted around to face Brayden.

"I feel like a selfish bastard," said Jamie.

"Rule of reality. Sometimes only one person gets off. Especially when it feels like I got mauled by a tiger. On the other hand, I am gonna make you clean your own mess." Brayden gave Jamie a teasing grin.

***

Half-drugged, in a brace that covered him from collar bones to hips, with strict instructions to not even think about getting out of bed, Steve Milbourne lay in Division P's infirmary making a pathetic attempt to read the email on his Blackberry. When the little electronic gadget rang, the vibration startled him enough that he nearly dropped it.

Glancing at the screen before he answered it, it read number blocked. "Milbourne," Steve said.

"This is Marcus Steele, I have good news and bad news for you."

"Regarding Jamie Ketelsen?"

"Of course."

"I'll take the good news first, because my day has been pretty abysmal," Steve replied.

"I heard it involved a bomb."

"Gee, news travels fast."

"Are you okay?" Steele asked. There was a note of sympathy in his voice.

"Not exactly. I broke a bone in my back."

"Holy fuck…I'm sorry. This will improve your day a little, though. I pulled in a couple favors from the DEA and it turns out they were doing some surveillance in the area where the car with Jamie's wallet was found. Somebody got a photo of the car as it passed. Two people were visible, both male, neither of them is Jamie. The photo was taken about ten hours before Jamie was found by your brother," said Steele.

"Keep going. It sounds like there's more," prompted Steve.

"So the story goes, this car pulls over into the parking lot that was being watched, and the second man gets out, exchanges a few words with the driver, aka the murder vic, then goes to another car in the lot as the driver pulls away. Car number two follows car number one several minutes later. The DEA considered the whole thing a little fishy but it didn't involve the people they were after so it just got filed away."

"This still doesn't prove Jamie was stashed in the trunk of the car or something along that line, but I guess it does offer another suspect for the murder," Steve said.

"We're waiting on Interpol to run the face of number two through their system."

"Can I get you to send me a copy of the photo? I have a suspicion he might be one of the people who tortured Jamie."

"Did his memory return?" asked Steele.

"Not really, just a few snips, but enough to help the forensic artist generate a sketch of one the kidnappers."

"Okay, I guess that's better than nothing. Can I come debrief Jamie? You've had a couple of days now to sort out his psychic thing."

Steve decided to hedge his bets a little. "Maybe tomorrow. I still need to check with the staff psychologist."

"I'm going to keep calling until you say yes, you know."

"I know and I expect that photo…" Steve pressed.

"I'll see what I can do."

***

Flash cards seemed amazingly low tech. Jamie looked across the small table at Sumiko. She had a stack of cards with letters of the alphabet. Blissfully they didn't have cutesy pictures on them as if they were designed for a child. He managed to get four out of twenty-six right. How lame was that.

"Wouldn't it be easier on both of us if you gave me a computer program to do this?" asked Jamie.

"Easier is not really the goal. In as much as this is a repetitive learning drill, Dr. Benford and I are still trying to get a full understanding of the damage done."

Jamie pointed at his temple. "Swiss cheese worse than a three day bourbon bender." He got up from the table and paced the room. He wanted out. He wanted to climb the walls. He felt so ridiculously dumb.

"Let's switch to numbers for a while," said Sumiko. She set out a different stack of cards.

Jamie forced himself to sit down again. "What does all this tell you, besides stupidly obvious crap, like I'm an adult that can't read or write any more?"

"Some of the things that are showing up are sequencing issues. You said you can't tie shoelaces. Your fine motor skills seem to be relatively intact, so it's not that your fingers are incapable, it's that your brain doesn't understand the order of the motions. Your speech and vocabulary are intact, but reading and writing use a different part of the brain. And I've read Stephen's preliminary reports and agree with him that the volatility of your emotions and hyper-excitability are a mix of PTSD and the actual neurological damage."

Jamie put his face in his hands for a moment. This was the most straightforward answer he'd gotten about what the hell was wrong with his brain. Slowly he lifted his head and looked at Sumiko.

"How much will I get back?"

"Of your actual life event memories? Some, but probably not all. Reading, writing, and other average daily tasks, I have the impression you'll get most of it."

"And how long will it take? Months? Years?"

"It's too early to tell. When I was doing some early rehab after my accident, I saw some stroke victims make great progress in just a few months."

Jamie stared bleakly at the table top. It seemed so impossible at this moment.

***

Seeing Steve in the enormous back brace, sitting very stiffly in a hospital bed, was disconcerting. Brayden crossed the room and sat on the edge of Steve's bed. "Trevor said you wanted to talk to me."

"I have some information about Jamie's case." Steve held out a tablet computer to him.

Brayden looked at the image.

"Meet Aben Nassar, a Syrian foreign national with suspected ties to one of the terrorist factions over there. He was last seen by the DEA roughly ten hours before you found Jamie. The DEA saw Nassar under suspicious circumstances. Facial recognition software places a ninety percent match between his photo and the sketch that Jennifer Sebastiano pulled from Jamie."

"So this is tied to CIA operations?"

"I'm not sure. Steele claims Jamie wasn't on assignment when this happened, but there's nothing to guarantee that somebody or other didn't blow Jamie's cover when he was overseas. These people have long and vicious memories."

"Still sounds kind of vague. What about charges against Jamie? Are they still pending?"

"Danny's been helping me try to sort out the legal end in case the CIA wants a scape-goat. We think we have a good case for insufficient evidence without having to get the Division P director to pull rank on the state's attorney."

"Okay, I guess that sounds promising. What comes next?" asked Brayden.

"I think we need to allow Marcus Steele to debrief Jamie, so maybe we can determine if this is linked to Jamie's recent assignments."

"This CIA guy is probably not going to let me sit in and keep an eye on Jamie, is he?" asked Brayden.

"Enh, we can ask, but I wouldn't bet on it."

***

A calm night, some sleep curled against Brayden, and a low key breakfast in the cafeteria left Jamie feeling about as ready as he was likely to be facing his CIA handler. He wished he knew something about his relationship with Steele. Were they friends? Did Steele trust him, or maybe more importantly did he trust Steele? What the hell had been the goal of the last assignment? He had a few brief memories of Ar Raqqah, Syria, and doing some kind of surveillance, but he didn't know who he had been watching or why.

He met Marcus Steele in one of the conferences rooms, and they shook hands. Jamie got the impression that perhaps he had trusted the man in the past. That was a good thing wasn't it?

"Have a seat." Marcus gestured toward one of the chairs along the table. "I'm glad to see you're up and around."

"The physical part's mostly healed," said Jamie. He pulled out the chair and sat.

Marcus sat facing him. "I know you've probably gone through a lot of testing and questions already, but I need to ask you some very specific ones."

"The memories of my life are mostly gone. I've regained a few, but it seems to be awfully random. Every now and then, something new will show up. Well, new to me now, I guess."

"What, if anything, do you remember of your last assignment?" Marcus asked.

"I have a couple memories of sitting in the niche of a balcony in Ar Raqqah, with a bitchin' long telephoto lens, taking pics of two guys talking in a café. I have no idea who they are or what they were discussing."

"We've been tracking an upsurge in arms dealing. Over the past couple of years several thefts have occurred from military bases, and we think there's an inside connection. There have also been a couple of attempts that failed. All the intel we've gathered so far points to a particular group that weirdly doesn't seem to have direct ties to any known terrorist factions. The intel itself though has been really thin. The men you were watching are suspected to have ties to the situation. Do you remember anything about the people who took you? Where? When?

"Nothing much really, there are just the couple of glimpses that the lady who does the sketches dug out of my head. The people I was watching; are they the ones who abducted me?" Jamie asked.

"I wish I could say yes, only because it would simplify things to a degree, but the people we traced with the sketches don't appear to have any connection other than one of them being Syrian. There are so many different factions operating in that country right now, I hesitate to say there's a verifiable link."

"Fabulous."

"We're still trying to trace the ring you saw, and see if there's an avenue to follow there," said Marcus. "In the meantime, I'd like to arrange for you to visit the site where the car was pulled out of the river. I spoke with Division P's psychologist, and he said there was a chance it might help you recover a few more memories. Would you be willing to try?"

Jamie took a deep breath and blew it out. Emotionally, he was less than thrilled with the idea but even with his seriously messed up brain he understood the need to try everything possible to put the pieces together. "Today?"

"No, I'd like to do it tomorrow if possible. I need to make sure all interactions with the Richmond police department are dealt with appropriately."

Jamie smiled a little. He knew from conversations with Brayden that Federal versus local law enforcement issues was sticky at best. A new thought occurred to him and he hesitated a moment before asking Steele. "With the explosion of Brayden's SUV and all, am I still in danger? And is Brayden for that matter."

"All I can say is maybe. We think the car bomb could very well be tied to your kidnapping. The forensic people say the bomb was a very simple affair, rigged to go off the next time the unlocking mechanism was triggered. There wasn't anything really unique or traceable about it. Our people think it may have been meant for you via your link to Brayden. Steve was just collateral damage.

"Is there a plan regarding my safety or Brayden's?"

"It's under discussion. For the moment, security here at Division P is more than adequate. The Richmond police have been told that Brayden is on loan to the federal government for an indefinite period of time while we try to resolve this." Marcus leaned back in his chair a little.

"And long term?"

"As yet to be decided."

Chapter 8

Steele and Valentine waited by the car while Jamie and Brayden walked along the river at the site where the car with the murder victim had gone in. Jamie was glad for Brayden's company and his silence. As he let his gaze roam over the grassy embankment, he saw the faint tracks where the car had been towed out of the water. They made a sort of logical sense but triggered no memories. What did he expect? A magic wand that would grant him back thirty-two years' worth of memories, as opposed to the tiny handful of fragments he currently possessed? He walked up the slope to the top. A light gust of wind blew across the dusty gravel edge of the road and the tickle that created at the back of his throat was suddenly choking.

He was dragged roughly from where he lay on the floor of the car's backseat, out onto dusty gravel. He dimly understood that this was the end. Somewhere amidst the aching confusion in his head, he knew this was his last chance. Lying face down on the stones, he felt a knife cut the zip-ties binding his ankles. That wasn't enough. The knife slid between his wrists and snapped through the tie there as well. He sensed the next slice was going to be his throat. Jamie flung himself onto his back and grabbed at his kidnapper's arms. They struggled for control of the blade, and it dipped close enough to Jamie's throat to touch the skin. He twisted hard and tried to head-butt his attacker, but the man blocked it with an elbow that struck Jamie in the side of the eye. Half-blinded, he wrenched again at the hand holding the knife, thrusting it between them and up… The knife sank into his assailant's belly with surprisingly little resistance and hot blood spilled across Jamie's naked chest. He struggled to push the dying man off of…

"Jamie! Jamie! It's not real!" a voice shouted.

Slowly Jamie became aware that he was lying flat on his back in the grass, and both Brayden and Marcus were holding him down.

"B-blood..." Jamie whispered.

"It was a memory babe, an awful fucking horrible memory," said Brayden, easing his hold.

"I stabbed him. He was going to kill me and dispose of my body and I was no more use and they were getting rid of me," Jamie babbled, words tumbling out.

"Don't, just don't." Brayden pressed a finger gently against Jamie's lips.

Jamie finally noticed Marcus hadn't moved a muscle. He was gripping Jamie's legs and staring fixedly at a spot in the vicinity of Jamie's ribs

Brayden followed Jamie's gaze and reached out to touch Marcus. "Hey, Steele?"

Marcus made a floundering flop across Jamie's legs, gasping. "Oh fucking God... he... you... knife... blood.." He was mumbling, face pasty white.

Danny, standing a step away, was the one who pulled the CIA handler back off Jamie's lower body. "I think he got an up close and personal view of Jamie's memory."

"But," Jamie began and didn't really know where to go with the half-formed thought.

"It happens sometimes. If the images are strong and traumatic enough, sometimes they can be broadcast to even the headblind," Danny commented. He gripped Steele by the shoulders. "Look at me, Marcus. Take a deep breath, and let it out slow."

Steele still looked thoroughly rattled. Danny helped the man to his feet and walked him back toward the car.

Jamie lay looking up at Brayden. He felt shattered. "I'm done. I'm just totally fucking done. Every time I try to shake loose my screwed up memories, only the bad shit falls out. No more. I'm finished!"

Brayden was silent, but he helped Jamie sit up and then sat on the grass facing Jamie, his hip against Jamie's.

Jamie leaned into Brayden's open arms. "He was going to cut my throat and dump me in the river," he whispered. "Something from my training… I don't know what, I think I did to him what he intended for me. Does that mean I've killed other people for the CIA?"

"I don't know," said Brayden. "I think you'd have to ask Steele about that, but Babe, I've killed two people in the line of duty, so even if you did, I don't think that makes you any different from me." Brayden rubbed Jamie's back. "Do you think you can stand up and walk?"

"Yeah, I think so. Jesus, one of these days maybe my brain will stop melting down every couple hours." Jamie slowly got to his feet.

Danny had taken Steele back to sit in the big SUV they had brought to the area. Now, Danny walked back toward Jamie and Brayden. "Are you okay? Should I call Peter?"

Jamie shook his head. "No, I'm fine, just another of my fucking hysterical freak outs."

"I've seen worse, in Iraq. Do you think you'll be able to give a statement for our records?"

Running fingers back through his hair, Jamie nodded. "Does all this stuff only go in Division P records? I'm just wondering because I think I'd have a really hard time explaining to The Company or DHS about the psi stuff and how you used kinda oddball methods to get what's left of my memories. I'm already feeling like a lab rat."

"For now, it stays with us. The CIA could request a copy, but generally speaking they tend to just nod and agree with whatever version we send them because the level of weird is too much for them," said Danny.

"God… There are moments when the level of weird feels like too much to me too," groused Jamie. "Are we done for today? Or maybe more importantly am I done for today."

Danny smiled. "Yeah, we're good."

Chapter Nine

The next day fell in the category of "filling in some blanks" and "wrapping up case elements". Too bad it didn't fill in any more blanks in Jamie's memory.

Information filtered in from Interpol. The dead man from the car was identified as a known Syrian terrorist on Interpol's watch list. This tidbit allowed the CIA to easily persuade the Richmond police that Jamie was truly a victim and no longer a suspect, not that the CIA divulged more than the bare minimum of information. This did, however, lead to the arrest of the accomplice seen in the DEA photos, who had bomb-making components in his motel room.

The CIA brass decided that further risk to Jamie was sufficiently low that he was free to pursue out-patient rehab with Division P for the next six months when a medical re-evaluation would occur.

"Did Benford or Valentine give you any idea of how the rehab thing is supposed to go?" asked Brayden.

Jamie glanced at Brayden as they walked along the pathway at Division P's complex. "Not really. Only that we'd take a break for the next few days and then set up some kind of a schedule. The rest is a kind of a see-how-it-goes thing, I guess."

"I'm finding it a little uncomfortable that the CIA is willing to leave you alone for a while. I mean, I know that they think the guy who set the bomb is in custody, and the guy who tried to off you is dead, but that still leaves unanswered questions."

Jamie heaved a sigh. "Leaving me alone and leaving me unwatched are not the same thing."

"You think they're going to keep tabs on you?"

"Yeah, I'd bet on it. I'm compromised, but how many people outside the agency know that? I think I'm a worm on a hook and they want to see if anybody bites."

Brayden threaded his fingers through Jamie's. "I'm not sure I'm thrilled with that idea."

Jamie's gut twisted and he painfully decided to offer Brayden an out. "You don't have to babysit me. I don't want to put you in more potential danger."

Brayden stopped walking and took hold of Jamie's shoulders. "Damn it, Jamie." He pulled Jamie tight to his body and kissed him passionately. Brayden opened up all his psi defenses. *I care about you. Fuck it. I think I love you. If you think I am going to let you push me away…* One of Brayden's hands cupped the back of Jamie's head.

Balling his hands in the fabric of Brayden's shirt, Jamie let himself lean against the warmth of Brayden's body. *I need you in my life so much. I just don't want you hurt because of me. Where do we go from here?*

"Forward," whispered Brayden. "The past is mostly gone even if not in the usual way. Unless Valentine or Steele is going to blow a gasket, I suggest we go to L.A. for a couple of days. Steve needs some help getting back out there and it's a convenient excuse to get the hell out of dodge for just a little while." He stared at the sky. Maybe he was hoping for divine help.

Jamie slid his arms around Brayden. "I could do with a few days of nobody but you in my head."

Epilogue

An unassuming, middle-aged man in an unremarkable car drove off the army base and down the street to a burger place under the guise of having lunch. Sitting in his car, he pulled out an inexpensive untraceable cell phone and dialed.

"Green," said the voice that answered. There was a slight accent to his voice.

"This is Mr. Brown. Did the package sell?"

"Yes."

"Good. And the man from P?"

"Damaged not dead, regrettably."

Brown stared through his windshield for a moment. "We have had far too much interference from them. Any useful information?"

"Some."

"Okay, keep on with the schedule. I'll be in touch." Mr. Brown ended the call, turned off the phone and removed the battery, putting it in his coat pocket.

Braided Lives

Danny Valentine is Division P's East Coast/International 'Fixer' and general go-to guy. He's had to come to terms with his bisexuality and his empathic abilities despite his military background. Peter Vithoulkas is Division P's immensely gifted healer, possessing one of the rarest of Talents. All fire and discipline, Peter is bisexual too, but it doesn't color his day-to-day reality until he spends some time under fire with Danny. Busy Danny and Peter fall into a 'friends with benefits' relationship that neither thinks much about.

Jennifer Sebastiano is an artist from a conservative family background who works part time as a forensic police artist. She spends a lot of time in crime victim's heads, seeing what they saw and helping them identify the criminals. It's Jen who shows Danny and Peter what they've really got between them. Danny and Peter think that Jen should be between them as well, but Jen isn't sure if she really fits there. As their three lives entwine, can Jen let go of societal and familial expectations? Can Danny and Peter convince Jen that there is a place for her in their unconventional relationship?

Hell Dogs Squadron

Navy F/A-18 pilot Lt. Cameron Bradshaw juggles a second government job in addition to his military commitments. He's a psychic finder for a mysterious agency known as Division P. Just as he starts the next Division P assignment, nearly lethal motorcycle accident nearly takes his life.

If not for the talents of gifted healer Dr. Mason Flynn, the Lt. might be dead. As the slow process of recovery begins, Mason Flynn is drawn to the injured pilot. A mix of shared psychic talents and physical attraction slowly binds them together, but the people responsible for Cam's accident escalate the affair, and soon Mason is running for his life.

A mad impromptu flight to Meridian Naval Air Station leads Cam and naval intelligence to a direct confrontation with a group of missile thieves. A vicious firefight leaves Mason scrambling to save teammates, but the final endgame forces Mason to do the unthinkable, and put his own sanity in jeopardy in the process. Can Cameron and Mason survive the trials thrown at them and their burgeoning relationship?

#3 in the Division P universe

Seeking the Balance

Lt. Cameron Bradshaw is an adrenaline junkie. You have to be to be a navy fighter pilot. It would never occur to him that his new lover, Dr. Mason Flynn, would think buying a new motorcycle to replace the one that was destroyed in his near fatal accident, was an insanely stupid idea. A vicious argument, an opportunity to cheat and some mistaken assumptions lead to worry and stress between the two men. A dying patient and assignment in Boston leads Cam and Mason to making choices that are both uncomfortable and difficult.

As Mason tries to come to terms with the concept of a patient he cannot save, seeing an old lover, and realizing that Cam Bradshaw's love for him may run deeper and stronger than he dared to hope all weave together into Mason working toward learning when it's time to let go of old fears.

Navy SEAL and Division P operative Jonas Nightengale is sent to Ft. Detrick, MD to determine who tried to divert a highly secret experimental missile. Sergeant Sarah Quilleran is in charge of security for the weapon and is overseeing the site where the missile landed-"in" the side of a cliff. While trying to use his psychic abilities (the talents that make him a part-time Division P agent) the two nearly fall from the cliff. Jonas saves Sarah's life and still manages to retrieve some information about the instigators of the security breach.

Sarah Quilleran is on emotional lock-down. She has spent her whole life denying that her psychic abilities are anything more than an occasional really accurate hunch. Her erratic, untrained gift often leaves her with either too much or too little information about the people around her. Things get sticky when the folks who want that weapon decide that they really want it, and are willing to do anything to get it. Will a bullet end the beginnings of Jonas' and Sarah's relationship?

Zero to 165

Most of the time life bumps along pretty predictably, viruses and vacations, Christmas and work issues, career and relationship choices. This is certainly true for part time Division P operatives Mason Flynn and Cameron Bradshaw. Mason is a doctor and a healer. Cam is a Navy pilot and a finder. Between building a life together and the stresses of managing both their part time and full time careers, life is pretty full for both guys. But sometimes, life throws a world-altering curve ball. Laws change. The past reaches out into the present and drops a miraculous bomb. Psychic stresses develop. People's realities alter in unpredictable ways. But Mason and Cam have each other even as their life grows in some very, very unexpected ways.

#6 in the Division P universe

Don't Fret the Timing

Secret Service agent Vaughn Breckenridge works the Treasury side of his agency. He's just been told that he's about to be evaluated for additional training. Sumiko Pierce isn't at all what he's expecting. She's testing for psychic abilities for the mysterious and near mythical Division P. Vaughn knows he's got an exceptional gut instinct, but he doesn't want to admit that it might be just a bit more than that. He doesn't have a clue what is about to hit him.

Sumiko Pierce is rebuilding her life after a devastating car accident left with her with serious injuries, some long-term, others healing slowly. It's hard enough to get around and do her job in a wheel-chair--even if it's only for a while. The last thing she needs is a hard-headed Secret Service agent pushing his way into her life in the same way she's pushing into his head. On the other hand, Vaughn's really attractive, inside and out.

He's got the abilities. She's got the abilities and the skills to teach him how to really start using those gifts. They are each going to have to let down their personal barriers in order to make it work. Will they manage it in time to save her life?

#7 in the Division P universe

Braided Lives 2: Splicing

Jennifer Sebastiano likes having control of her life. As a psychic, more control is always better. Her lovers, Danny Valentine and Peter Vthoulkas feel pretty much the same way for similar reasons. But life has a way of turning sideways for everybody, even Division P operatives--maybe especially Division P operatives. When Danny's mental protections start to fail and Jen runs into a mugger, Peter's suddenly got his hands full. As their lives get complicated, none of the three likes living four or five hours apart, but Jen isn't sure she wants to turn her life completely upside down to move nearer the guys either. Why is it always the woman who has to upend her universe when relationships get serious? Now life has dumped a whole lot of trouble into their laps and the three of them have to figure out how to handle it all. These are the sorts of issues that either pull lovers closer together--or split them apart. And it's pretty much up to Jen to decide which it will be.

#8 in the Division P universe

Begin and End with You

Late one night, while driving home after a shift, Richmond City Detective Brayden Milbourne, finds a man stumbling alongside the road, bloody and confused. Shocking enough to find him; more shocking is that Brayden knows the man. He and Jamie Ketelsen had hooked up during a memorable weekend not long ago.

Fun then, but now, Jamie is a CIA field agent with a major problem. He can't remember his name or how he got on that dark road. He doesn't remember Brayden either. The situation only gets more complicated when it becomes obvious that Division P, the government agency that deals with psychic agents, needs to be involved.

Can a man who only has the present connect with a man who might have to arrest him for his forgotten and dangerous past?

#9 in the Division P universe

The LD50 of Memories

Navy Pilot Cameron Bradshaw and orthopedic surgeon Mason Flynn are fast working towards solidifying their new family. But life is full of bumps and bruises-- from a sudden lack of diapers for their daughter to Mason's bigoted father passing away. Cam is having scary psychic shock episodes too. After a terrible experience doing a Division P body-finding job, Cam's shields crash hard and he suffers life threatening physical side effects. The solution complicates their lives further. Still, between Jane, their new nanny, and the men reconnecting with an adult sibling apiece, they can see their new family forming around them. Maybe it's time to make it all official?

#10 in the Division P universe

Fragmentation

Shea Bradshaw wakes up after a party with memory loss, ill and in someone else's bed--and there are two more people in the bed with him. Shea is Navy EOD, on detail in Norfolk after the death of his partner during the defusing of an IED in Afghanistan. Shea's head is not in a good place; he's suicidal. In addition, his telekinetic abilities seem to be reacting badly to his emotional stress. Like his brother Cam, Shea is psi. He keeps it a secret, though it can't stay that way much longer. Every flashback and emotional crisis results in severe TK incidents.

Lynn Bayliss is an ex-military interrogator with issues of her own. Skip Monacheke is a State cop. The two of them have a "friends with benefits thing" going on and they like to share occasionally. When they rescue Shea from a drugged drink at that party and then can't get any sort of coherence from him, they take him home; they have no idea what they are about to let themselves in for. There are secrets and psi all around. Shea needs help and Cam, Shea's brother, has Division P as a resource. But someone's gunning for Division P and it all gets tangled together. Can three people find their way to each other in the middle of chaos and crises?

#11 in the Division P universe

Braided Lives 3: Tangles

Coming in 2021